Don't Cross the Devil

by

Cameron H. Chambers

Also by Cameron H. Chambers

For the Love of a Madman

The Stone Cabin

Confessions of an Internet Don Juan

To those that love unconditionally…

"I made this simple prayer to God. Make my enemies foolish."

Voltaire

Chapter One

"What's with the bird?" Silka said.

"Early warning. He can see spirits come in and out of the room. He squawks when they do."

"I see. Does he have a name?"

"Snooker," I said.

"Snooker—as in to snooker someone, or the billiards game?"

"Oh, you've played?"

"I've played before."

"My, my, an accomplished billiards player yet. I should have guessed. You grow more interesting by the hour," I said.

"How can you tell that I am good?" Silka asked.

"If someone is a shark, he never lets on from the get go, and if someone is a lousy pool player, he says he is lousy because he doesn't want to be taken for a shark, if by chance he is much better than his opponent. If someone is good, but not a shark, he, or she in your case, won't make it sound like she is so very good because one never quite knows the level of abilities with whom she is speaking or playing. I find you interesting. What else do you do?" I said.

"Well, I see no subtlety is lost on you. I don't know. You'll find out, I guess: if there is some reason for you to."

"I have no plans to go anywhere. You may be the one," I said.

"The one what?" Silka said.

"The one that saves me."

"How's that pot roast coming?" she said.

I had met Silka first in a dream and next while getting coffee at what became our favorite bistro. We became acquainted when she lived above me in the shabby apartments I moved into after I was forced to leave my wife. She helped me move, in fact, or rather she would have helped me move. She did help with a few little odds and ends. It was tense seeing my wife again and so soon after what she had done to me. To have a young, pretty gal in her early thirties at my side was a fortunate circumstance for me, and an excellent way to rub salt in my wife's pustule of an open wound upon failing to kill me, but in all, it was most unpleasant to be so burdened with a woman, and I mean my wife, who was destined to finally, after needless years of union, become my ex-wife.

Silka was a thin, gangly woman with dangerous good looks and an intent gaze, which either masked a secretive anger or some underlying fear. I could not tell which really. She was complex and a good lover. She did not go on about things easily, nor was she one to complain much. I learned immediately that she was a good poker player and had a head for numbers. She enjoyed bluffing, but I am difficult to bluff, and am not hoodwinked often by fabrications. Silka did, as a routine matter of course, keep matters tucked tightly in her vest. That was prudent as I saw it.

She was from the Midwest, somewhere in Kansas, a small town named Hiawatha I believe, near the Missouri border, the "Show Me State," an hour and a half or so north of Kansas City. She spoke plainly and without accent, as it is with true Midwesterners, and was the only daughter and had six siblings. Her parents had farmed and raised hogs like their parents before them and on the same plot of land. She described her parents as a simple lot not unintelligent, just unsophisticated, as they had no need of sophistication or putting on airs. Silka was a practical woman in need of some refinement and more formal education herself. She was well read; however, the nights on a farm are lonely without a partner. She had enjoyed only one or two boyfriends in her years and the affairs had not ended well. She seemed afraid of venturing forth too much, or rather more precisely of being left behind.

I found Silka clear of mind and an independent woman, self-assured and understanding except for that irksome knowing look she would shoot me frequently, when it was more likely the case she knew nothing of what I spoke. She did not believe in much I said either, thought it some sort of wild tale, but thankfully knew almost no one here besides me and found my intricacies of personality appealing. For Silka, my reputation did not precede me, which was good luck on my part. I needed for her to believe in me, if, in fact, she was the one. I had no way of being certain she was or when I might discover the necessary information about her.

She had landed near Orlando, Florida. I was from here and well known in my city, owing to my artistry chiefly, popular paintings and sketches of my life and surroundings. That's not the only reason I am well known. I have led a rough, coarse life and have many detractors, foes even, I would call them. There are those among my city, witless, vapid drones, waiting earnestly to spit on my grave. Or perhaps put me there. They would enjoy such notoriety, I think. I am cautious and paranoid, and I am shrewd or would long ago be dead. I suppose there will be a great celebration in my city upon my passing. I would have nothing less.

When Silka's parents died not too long ago, and her brothers wanted to sell the farm, she agreed and took her one-seventh of the inheritance. Requiring warmer weather, she moved first to Tampa and was washed out of her home twice in the same season by hurricanes. She moved inland and had only been in Orlando a brief while when I met her.

It was at a specialty store, famous for its coffee and delicacies. I darken the doors of coffee shops frequently. I find the air conducive to conversation though I am some-times silent in public. If I am not deep into my art or meditation of my art, I have virtually nothing to do, so a café au lait is a welcome diversion. Divorced, with no children, no close relations nearby and a small smattering of acquaintances, and none I can call friend, I am now the lone wolf that preys upon the interesting or unusual looking in search of fertile conversation, and I am disappointed most days. On occasion I say, "thank you," and "you're welcome," or if in a good mood, "let me get that," and nothing more on my behalf. I am not the socially graceful creature like my father. Polite yes, to a tee, because it suits me, and it keeps the critics at bay. I am weary of their inane comments, their childish prattle and their endless speculation. I have been dealt with very harshly all my life and I rarely engage a stranger in chit-chat unless it suits me. I am suspicious of them, scared and untrusting and afraid of what I might do. But Silka was different.

She was wearing a zippered jacket, open to just below her nubile breasts, and she wore a green midriff and Capri pants, which belied her shapely figure and her age as somewhere around thirty. She sat at a counter by herself, sipping a plain coffee and she sported long blonde hair, unnaturally straightened, a hint of oily skin and a honey-scented perfume. I spotted her upon entering, though the inside of the coffee shop was dimly lit.

I have a sense for most things. It is greater than mere instinct, but I do not diminish the role of instinct. Instinct has saved my life before. Sometimes dramas play out in my mind seconds before they ultimately come true, or if the matter is of sufficient import, I will have a vision long before the encounter, whether physical or spiritual. I am clairvoyant and clairaudient. Silka had visited me as an apparition from an ethereal plane just the night before. At what became our favorite hangout, her long legs dangled from a high wooden stool, here and there touching and balancing on her tiptoes on the hard surface of the floor, decorated in some elaborate Mediterranean tile, and she looked with keen interest at a magazine.

I assumed it was a fashion or interior design magazine or of some such ilk; young women her age seemed so superfluously distracted nowadays, but the magazine was on finance and the stock market, subjects close to my heart. It was an issue I was familiar with.

"Did you read the article on the professionally managed exchange traded funds?" I asked.

"Excuse me?" she said, seeming a little annoyed that I had interrupted her reading or possibly she was just taken aback by a strange man.

"The last article…it's on global, professionally managed ETFs?"

"I'm sort of new at this," Silka said. "I don't know what an ETF is."

"I won't presume to explain. It's a good article. Very informative."

"Are you a broker?" Silka inquired.

"No. I'm more of a bum. I paint if that counts."

"Well, I suppose it does. But how do you feed your family?"

"Oh, no family. Just me really. And I do all right with it. I'm married at the moment, but I guess I'm going through a divorce. I guess I have been for quite some time. Years, perhaps. The latest incident brought things home to me."

"What happened?" Silka asked, laying her magazine to rest for the moment.

The plane slid into the runway at Kastrup, Copenhagen's largest airport. It is the twentieth largest airport or so in the world. The runway was icy, but that didn't seem to bother anyone, least of all the pilots. I felt us slip sharply to the left as the landing gear impacted the frozen-over tarmac, but the pilot immediately corrected, suspecting what might happen, having dealt with these conditions so many times before. He made a rather blasé gesture of calm to his passengers, by saying "A bit of an ice patch is all. The time in Copenhagen is 7:00 a.m. The temperature is -12 degrees. Enjoy your stay." The words were immediately translated into English by a stewardess, an American woman in her thirties, but my Danish was sufficient and I had understood. I knew we had left JFK the day before around 6:00 in the evening, and the aforementioned temperature of -12 would be about 10 degrees Fahrenheit, quite cold for a Florida-born tourist.

I could see snow flurries as we taxied the short distance to our gate, and my wife and I stepped off the plane and were in Denmark. Why she had dragged me here in January on such short notice was a mystery to me. I had been informed that we had swapped houses with a Danish lady and her two kids that wanted to see Disney. Florida makes a leading choice for swapping homes, which is a relatively inexpensive way to visit overseas. It would have been our first house swap, but my wife had lied about all the details from the beginning. She was clever that way. So there was no house swap. There was no Danish lady and her two kids winging their way to our home in Orlando, the children feverishly awaiting the magic of Disney. And what was worse—I did not see a thing coming. That was somewhat unusual.

I had no idea whose grimy, squalid apartment we were about to visit. Alison, my wife of nine years, had chat connections from around the world; wherever the Internet extended its treacherous reach, Alison had a friend or accomplice there who usually had misconceptions about meeting my comely wife. She did not know these people well, nor did she care what type of person they were; she cared only how easy it was to lead them on and how carefully they would execute her bidding.

We gathered our luggage and took a taxi to the Kongens Enghave district, a not so charming part of Copenhagen known for great numbers of destitute young single mothers and the unemployed. Like much of Europe has become, Denmark is in many ways a welfare state with its own separate black market economy. I started to feel uneasy about where we were going and the area, so I questioned my wife, but she feigned ignorance on the short ride over from the airport. My wife and I were not wealthy, though we possessed some financial wherewithal, but neither were we complete snobs; the area we were traversing was clearly not our element.

Kongens Enghave, or King's Meadow, is about ten kilometers from the international airport. It was built with the optimism of becoming a substantial residential area, once with smart-looking four-story brick apartment buildings, but quickly became overrun by those in need of government aid, poor immigrants who did not speak the language and a seedier aspect. Commerce abandoned the district and unemployment remains a problem.

It was our only trip to Copenhagen. I had recently sold an original of one of my finer works to a film producer at a showing at my manager's gallery in Orlando, and since my wife insisted she had swapped out our comfortable home in the suburbs, and we were contract bound to clear out of our house, we might as well see what Copenhagen offered. Naturally, she had me pay for the first class airline tickets. And she knew very well I could be enticed to visit almost anywhere by the great wanderlust in my soul. That is a characteristic I share with my father. The driver left us on a corner and pointed to our destination. I think he wanted to exit the area quickly though crime is not really much of a problem in Denmark. I paid him the twelve Euros for the short ride and lugged mine and my wife's bags amid worsening snow and skies down the frozen path.

Remarkably, she had a key to the door. She claimed the lady with the two kids had sent it to her in the mail. I knew that was not how it was done. My senses were aroused. If a swap had taken place, we would have needed to pick up the key at an agency of some sort. I wondered, in retrospect, if an exchange had been made while we were in JFK. Perhaps she actually met someone who lived here in Copenhagen, and possibly this apartment we were about to enter belonged to him or her. I knew to keep my eyes on my wife at all times, but she was very cunning. My wife was not a smart woman, or well educated, but made up for it by her deviousness and ability to convincingly disavow knowledge of anything untoward. She was a brilliant actor.

We passed through a metal exterior door, and she led us into a dark apartment with a barely discernible and vulgar décor. The couple of sticks of furniture gave out a negligible air and the bathroom smelled of urine and feces. She insisted we nap immediately after the long flight, and that in a few hours we could get something to eat and look around the city. She was adamant that I could have the side of the bed closest to the radiator, which was turned on high and lodged carelessly against the bed frame.

I fell asleep quickly, but my snores stirred me into consciousness, albeit a tepid reasoning, foggy and cloudy. I was out maybe several minutes, and having slept heavily, and when I awoke I was handcuffed to the radiator. My wife was gone, and the door to the apartment was closed. The blankets that substituted for shades were drawn tightly over the solitary window, and no lights were on in the tiny apartment. The radiator was turned off and the knob was in a position so that I could not reach it to turn it on again. There was no heat in what was basically one room and a bath, and I was shivering.

Then just moments later, as I began to realize what was happening to me, a radio that had been set to automatic began blaring some kind of odious electronic techno music at an intense volume. It drowned out the irritating cries of the babies I had heard earlier upon entering the tenement. The volume was so intense, in fact, that I could not be heard, when I yelled over the din for help, and I gathered quickly that no one would care about the noise, or that this might be a usual circumstance and of little concern. By then fully awake, I understood something that panicked me, which heretofore I had remained calm, although was losing my composure bit by bit. The stove was left on and I could smell and then hear, during a space of dead air on the radio, the gas filling the tiny apartment. The gas smelled like rotten eggs and there was a faint hiss of derision that accompanied its escape. I had no choice, so I reluctantly prayed to my father.

During this break in the music from the radio, an obvious flaw in the plan that might have let a lesser man's cries of desperation form an awareness of the need for action or duty in a Good Samaritan's heart, I could hear a man laughing from the far end of the hall. This was no ordinary man.

"Would you like to help your son?" I asked.

The radio's white noise hummed menacingly like lapping flames, but I could then hear the goings on down the hall. There were two loud bangs on a door that must have been several apartments removed from the one I was in. I heard the man's voice say he was going to cut off the woman's gas if she did not pay her bill. The conversation was in Danish, but I could make out most of it. What I could not understand in the Danish language came across to me in English, a sort of built-in language translator of mine, very convenient, so I was able to remain current with the unfolding act. The young woman pleaded with the man not to cut her gas, stating she had small children and no husband, and she needed to feed her babies. The man laughed and called her a whore and said he was going to turn off the gas to the entire building and throw the whole lot of squatters, as he called them, out on the street and get new tenants. She cursed the man, calling him "demos," or demon in Danish, and she slammed the door in a flurry of sobs. Just after that, the gas in the room, where I was trapped, shut off.

    "You're on your own from here, buddy-boy," I heard the man say as he walked down the hall. He laughed again. It was neither a cruel nor affable laugh, more a laugh belonging to a mildly disinterested yet amused party, and I could hear him zip up his down vest noisily at the end of the hall, go through the metal door and enter the street.

Chapter Two

"There he is. He's going into an attorney's office. It's a divorce attorney," a man in his late forties or early fifties said. He was staring in my direction from his position leaning over a nearby balcony, talking into a cell phone, and I returned his gaze, upon which he said, "He heard me. Gotta go." He then disappeared inside a building.

I had heard most of the peculiar man's end of his cell phone conversation once I pulled up into the half-empty parking lot. I was not sure why anyone cared what I did. I am noteworthy, but a minor figure in my city at best. The man did not look like a detective or a law enforcement type—that much was welcome news. I kept my act clean. I do not enjoy the company of cops in professional matters that are of their concern and greatly prefer to settle any exigency that may arise on my own. I have been in a few tussles here and there, but not one of them had I started, and the other guy always had it coming. Police officers usually look the other way in situations such as these, and mediation, if court entanglements look likely, works well if postponed until the parties involved have had a cooling-off period. Attorneys I find more necessary and useful to me than the police.

I hear things from time to time. It may come as a voice, an audible and resonating thought from a deep crevasse inside my mind, or the discomforting and alarmed cries of a bird or squirrel, or the melodious notice of a wind chime perhaps, which alert me to this or that, and give me directions or instructions on various matters. The vibrations feel like a bit of pressure or sensation within and have helped me to avoid many landmines. This encounter with the man on his cell phone, obviously not a chance one, was a tiny tidbit of information gleaned for my own good from a more external source. My timing rarely falters. But I had been shown the man on the cell phone for an unusual and as yet unexplained reason.

When some odd thing occurs in my life and there is no apparent cause, I know it is not the work of ghosts or goblins, but rather by design of humans. Most would think science would be the answer to some inexplicable phenomena, and some inkling of knowledge they are not privy to, but I can always discern the human element. I clearly am able to feel the spirits that bump around and play their games and tricks. I hear them frequently in my mind or ears or sense them in my mind's ears and eyes. And the man on the cell phone was no spirit. In this case, someone was keeping tabs on me, I gathered, and I had no real way at present of knowing who it was or why I might be a subject of interest, but then it mattered less to me than I may make it sound.

I had pulled up in my car for an eleven o'clock appointment with Reggie Tate, esquire. He dealt in extractions of the marital kind, and I had ample reason now to end my long-standing charade of a union with my wife. I sat in my car for a moment and reflected.

I ran into Silka again not long after our discussion over coffee. It was the next day and I was entering my building, where I had relocated, and I could not have counted myself luckier to learn she and I were nearly neighbors. It was not that I had a habit of jumping into things with women, but occasionally I did, as opportunity to do so came my way often, and frequently it worked out satisfactorily for a time between us. I was a bit of a lady's man, though pushing fifty, but with a full crop of graying black hair and an athletic body, and a reputation for treating women like the precious metals they are.

Silka had a palpable style about her—young, but certainly not overly carefree or invincible in thought or deed, and perhaps a light spirit most of the time, but she clearly was hiding some uncomfortable secret. She lived in the same-side apartment on the floor above me. My first night in my new apartment I also could distinguish her hip hop and reggae music; they were bands I was unfamiliar with, and I heard also the sexually-charged lyrics and rhythms she listened to were accompanied by her odious sobbing until she fell asleep. I did not know at first the woman on the crying jag in the apartment above me was Silka. I assumed it was a jilted lover. She sounded tormented over something I was sure had to do with human relations. They were not the laments of the spiritually oppressed, at least not the tears of one oppressed by the spirits themselves, but definitely the woman above me had a soul that struggled against subjugation.

Just prior to that day of mine and Silka's meeting, I had met a dull, witless gal named Renee who was generously endowed and possessed large teeth with an unmistakable and equally impressive gap between her two uppers, and she had an available apartment for me, so I prepared to move in. We went back to the office so I could sign the lease, and playing on the radio, turned up loudly, a song belted from the shiny, mystical box: "Room 16 ain't got no view, but the hot plate's brand new, I guess I showed her." I determined that my father had learned of my whereabouts already. He kept track of me often, much more of late, though he interfered in my life less and less, unless he felt he had a reason.

The apartment complex was run down. The outside and inside lights above the transom to the entrance of my building were burned out, and the paint had mostly peeled off the door and the inside walls of the foyer, leaving a flecked decaying green tint. Part of the lawn in front of my building was uncut and looked like it had been in that condition for some time. I gathered the managers had a tough time hanging onto employees. Even in Florida, where rent and expenses are cheaper than most of the country, it is difficult to live on minimum wage. I always hear the comment, "I can't get out of bed for that pay."

It was a different side of town for me, off State Route 17 in a pocket of ghetto surrounded by the otherwise pleasant Altamonte Springs area, near the local hangout for teens, the "CrackDonalds" and other fine eateries. I was certain no one would look for me here. Silka and I had bumped into each other as I carried up my groceries and as she descended the roughly carpeted stairs with exposed tacks poking mischievously up on the sides, and she was apparently in a hurry.

"Hey there," I said. I was surprised to see her, but not entirely.

"Oh, hey. Chris, right? Do you live here?" she asked. Not noticing at first it was I who had said hello, she had kept walking down the stairs, and her countenance was slumped possibly hiding tearful eyes, and then she stopped on the third rung down from me. She slyly wiped her eyes before facing me as she spun around, but was caught short for something clever to say, and she seemed agitated and glanced toward the outside door.

"Are you in a hurry? I'm going to make pot roast," I said.

"I am. I am in a hurry, but it won't take long. Which one are you?"

"12 C. Second floor."

"I'll stop by later, if that's okay?" Silka said.

"Sure."

I got out of my car and walked into my attorney's office. Reggie was a younger man than I. He was dressed in a navy blue cardigan with a navy blue tie, affixed carelessly, and pressed dark trousers and black shoes. We exchanged greetings and he got immediately to the heart of the matter.

"My fee, Mr. Devin, is fifteen hundred and filing is another three hundred, as long as there is no contest. If your wife contests the divorce, which rarely happens, I bill at one hundred and fifty dollars an hour. I will be there to represent you in court. It is a simple proceeding. Your wife doesn't even have to come. I will need disclosure of all assets. You mentioned over the phone there are no children?"

"Right, no children. We were expecting twin girls, but we lost them." I could not fathom what compelled me to tell Reggie about the loss of my unborn children. I suppose my wife's hostility and rage that resulted from the loss of her impending offspring were the real reasons my marriage deteriorated into a sham, and I further suppose it was the reason my wife now wished me dead. And perhaps, of course, there might be a clandestine insurance policy taken out on me floating around with her as beneficiary. My signature would be forged, of course. My wife's motives always ran to money. She was very singleminded of purpose.

Our unborn children's demise, and my wife Alison ending up childless, was only partly my fault. Alison and I had lived together for just six months before we got married, and she had gotten pregnant by me during that time. I had no idea I had caused the pregnancy. I had never gotten a woman pregnant before I was reasonably assured, and as I was in my late thirties at the time of the pregnancy, I did not think I was able to get a woman pregnant, owing most likely, I thought, to a number of sports-related injuries from college.

What was more, I felt Alison had orchestrated and manipulated the affair, hoping to surprise me with hopeful good news of a son or daughter on the way. To make matters much worse, Alison had married another man and had gotten hitched during the time she and I were beginning our relationship and Alison kept it a secret from me. She was a bigamist. He was a foul-breathed, low-browed immigrant, not that I have anything against men or women of foreign extraction; I don't at all, nor really against anyone, but he never worked and spent most of his time bouncing around bars and jail cells. Alison had needed money she claimed in her defense.

The man was not from a bad family as it turned out, and he had a rich uncle who was able to pull some strings for him and get him a work visa in America. This altruistic act was to keep the man out of prison in his own country and to send him away to a new land and protect the family's reputation. He was living in Orlando and his visa would soon expire, and rather than live in America illegally or face possible deportation, which neither he nor any member of his family wanted, he was instructed to find a girl to marry. Somehow he met Alison and convinced my new girlfriend to marry him and that he allegedly would pay her several thousand dollars for doing so.

She planned to never tell me of her liaison. She thought she would string me along, a suffering artist with limited funds, but one with a modicum of potential and reasonably easily controlled by a stronger, more forceful personality, which Alison represented at that time, and if it looked like marriage between us she could get a divorce and I would be none the wiser. But she did not bother to divorce him. If things did not work out with me, she could remain married to the foreign man and keep him on the hook for several years' worth of payments. This I believe was the plan that had been hatched, but I have no certain knowledge of it being so.

But Alison was not a discreet woman. I caught the two of them talking in our kitchen when she did not know I was home. I had put my car in the shop and gotten a ride home, and upon failing to see my car in the driveway, she assumed I was absent from our rather spacious house. The man never paid her any money, so I was told, and he claimed, when he and I almost came to blows in my kitchen, that it was his child Alison was carrying. She had not as yet told me she was pregnant, and apparently was unsure to whom the child belonged. Not one of us knew at the time it was twins. I am uncertain if Alison knows today. I never told her of the fact it was twins or told her how I came across that information.

I informed Alison that if she had the baby I would leave her. I believed the man when he claimed it was his baby. This affair of theirs could have been a longstanding relationship for all I knew at the time. I was not going to put up with another man's baby, especially his. It was revealed to me early in our relationship, mine and Alison's, through a vision that the pregnancy was caused by me and if it had been fruitful it would have born twins, two identical girls, but Alison had aborted the fetuses. The spirits of the twins have chosen to reside with me. I hear them laughing on occasion, the mirth of children, happy ones usually, as somehow in the process they must have grown to a certain age. I'm not certain what I will do if they become teenagers. I think they have forgiven me for my part. Alison has never mentioned hearing them: she is not prone to voices.

Alison never so much as got a blood test. I never directly asked her to do what she did, as even then I was looking for a way out of, "*un affaire de passion*," and I assumed she would elect to continue her pregnancy and extricate herself from me, not her future offspring. What woman would not given the circumstances? I was wrong in judging Alison's character from the start. She saw dollar signs, so she terminated the pregnancy. I then felt I had no choice but to marry her, as guilt was a weapon Alison wielded mightily, and further stick by her side, defend her even. I deeply regretted telling my wife I would leave her if she had the baby, or babies as the case may be, and I learned to regret meeting Alison altogether and marrying her and staying with her for nine years.

I remember my father saying once of his unhappy union to my mother that he lamented his marriage from early on, which in the case of my parents lasted twenty-six years. He had believed in his vows obviously with my mother, at least for a time. His second wife was not so fortunate. It is not easy to hear that about one's mother, that she was considered woefully inadequate as a partner. My father had added he hoped my marriage was brief and I would not look back on it much. He did so not to spoil the broth or overturn my cart but in an earnest statement of caring and concern for me, which was a rarity at best from him. But I know him and of him in many different ways than most understand him.

"I assume the two of you have a house," Reggie said.

"Yes. She'll want to keep it. She can refinance it, pay me my half, and keep it in her name."

"If that's agreeable, then fine. I will need the three hundred for the filing fee up front. You need to think about the items in the home you want to keep. I can have us a court date within six to eight weeks."

I wrote out the check to Reggie Tate and got up to leave. I closed the door behind me and walked into the relentless Florida sun and out to the still half-empty parking lot. Even in January, the sun screamed down upon the unwary with its blinding light, making everything a little more intense and insensible. The light hurt my eyes as it was a very bright day, and I already felt the growing reduction in the restorative effects of the rays; this gradual loss of beneficial light would continue until next season. I require an intensity of the sun's rays; the brightness is only one aspect and more of a nuisance than anything in Florida. Aside from vitamin D and a kicker for photosynthesis there are many things in sunlight that the scientists have yet to discover. As there are fewer of these shards of beneficial light since the sun is farther away on its axis from the northern hemisphere in winter, it was likely I would become increasingly more miserable until spring. I would suggest the pieces of what is not known about sunlight have to do with mood and mood stabilizers, which I suspect are actual organic substances in the light itself. Coming off a terrible holiday season, my anger and rage were likely to compound until spring.

There was a knock at the door. I knew it had to be Silka. I didn't think the maintenance man for the apartments, if there was one, would be working in the early evening, and he or she, if such a creature existed, I guessed would probably not know I had taken possession of my apartment, nor was he likely to care if he had been so informed. This was not the kind of building where the door man or a concierge buzzed the occupant begging permission to allow a visitor up or eager employees hustled to fix a problem. There was no phone yet, and I noticed there was no intercom. I assumed my mailbox, which I had the key to, would have leftovers and solicitations in it.

"Hi," I said as I opened the door and welcomed my guest in. "I know it does not look like much, but it's really nothing at all." I was indicating to my latest acquaintance, which was plain enough for her eyes, that there was not a stitch of furniture anywhere to be seen. Not a tapestry or painting adorned the walls of my new abode and a huge dark discoloration, probably the business of a large dog, further marked the threadbare carpet as being old and worn out. The walls were freshly painted and there was no odor other than what was coming from the kitchen, and it was not a disagreeable stench, but rather the night's supper.

"I like what you've done. You're a minimalist, I see," Silka said.

"Actually, I'm a realist. In art and life. I had a cooking pot, a set of plastic plates, knives and forks, and a change of clothes in the trunk of my car. We don't have any napkins, however. And I don't have a towel. Dinner should be ready in about fifteen minutes. I hope you like pot roast. You are staying for dinner, of course."

"How are you going to sleep tonight?"

"Knees up, butt on the floor, elbows on my knees, head in my hands and my back to the wall. Bandito-style. I was a Mexican gunslinger in a past life. Your meeting went well?" I asked.

Silka's countenance had greatly brightened since I had last seen her and I noticed she had reapplied her makeup after what I assumed was another of her soulful cries. A hint of a smile graced her thin lips and there was more of fun in her demeanor. I knew instinctively she was hiding something but that she felt better for the moment, so I would not press her for knowledge of her problem, as we were new to each other and I saw something of a future for us already. But there was something very wrong in her life and I did not know what it was, nor did I feel it prudent to ask just yet. I was not certain I wanted to know at all. I deemed the matter had import for me, but it would either resolve itself or I would learn of its aspect. Were Silka my soon-to-be ex-wife I would know the matter dealt with money, either money she owed to someone or money she could not collect that was owed to her. With Silka, I felt this had more to do with the human heart.

"Oh yes, thank you for asking," Silka said. "A small misunderstanding to take care of. That's all."

She had a puzzled look momentarily, not from the question I asked, but rather I could see her mind working, laboring ever so slightly as though a new opportunity had appeared on the horizon, and she was uncertain what to make of it. I have seen that look dozens of times. The expression is a cross between the realization of a pleasant surprise and some good fortune perhaps, and a bit of reticence and disbelief. Women are exquisitely complex, I find.

Men are more like switches or triggers. They come alive, fire and turn off until reactivated. Men are sometimes more reactionary than women. The minds of most women are something like a state of constant motion, or in a condition of zero gravity where inertia actually keeps them in play and they blink and whir and light up constantly; minds that never rest, and if the woman is experienced or well-educated, good ideas pour forth more regularly than from a man's mind of comparable proclivities. But the world is brutal and aggressive, and not always a fair spot for just any woman, yet a man with cunning and purpose will not be denied his place in it. I am not a cunning man. I am without guile. But I am shrewd and have insights that keep me out of harm's way. I have always felt though that I will come to a tragic, possibly violent end. But I have always felt too that it has to be that way or I can never be reborn out of my precarious situation.

The timer on the stove went off like a gunshot, signifying our meal was ready. Silka announced she would return in a moment's notice, and she did so with a roll of paper towels, a bath towel, a bar of soap and a partially empty container of shampoo. The items were welcome additions to my new home.

"So, you've told me a little about your life with your parents. Why did your brothers want to sell the farm?" I asked.

"It was too much work for everyone. I have six brothers. I am the second eldest in my family and my one brother, the eldest, pretty much calls the shots. Mom and dad had both been ill for a long time. He had throat cancer and she had rheumatoid arthritis. I watched them work so hard every day of their lives until they just couldn't anymore. I watched my brothers as well. My youngest brother got to go to college, but mom and dad wanted to keep me with them. They wanted me to do the accounting, sales and taxes. And they needed my brothers to work the land. Two of my younger brothers had always wanted to move to Kansas City, and they got the chance eventually, and the eldest could not run things without them. We all worked very hard, but we couldn't keep up as our parents had, so my brother wanted to sell while we still could. I got some money, but none of us got as much as we thought we would. And then we had sold the farm and are now without it. In retrospect, we probably should have hired a manager."

Snooker, my parakeet, was quiet during dinner. I did not enjoy being without my bird, especially in public places, and that was where I could not take him, his cage being oversized and difficult to carry around. Few establishments too welcome a bird, and he is quite noisy at times. He was the only thing I grabbed when I left my home, not even the contents of my safe. I noticed the air in my apartment had changed perceptibly and was less forbidding. I could feel the robust and vital energy pouring forth from my dinner guest and it was relaxing and fresh for me. Perhaps she had resolved something in her life or made peace with it. She became obviously more comfortable as we progressed with our meal. I wondered if she would cry herself to sleep again that night. We chatted on about Florida, farms, colleges, a bit of a sore topic I found, and a variety of matters that were interesting to me. My mother had grown up on a farm outside of St. Louis. I had spent many a summer in the Midwest with her relatives.

"So your parents did not want you to marry?" I asked.

"They were not opposed to the idea, but they did not want me to leave home, so I didn't. Their health had been touchy even before they grew ill and died. There were not many boys left in my little town either. The smart ones all went off to bigger cities. Other than a few months in Tampa, this is my first time being away from home, and my first time living alone. I don't like it much. It's noisy and quiet at the same time," Silka said.

"I'm not big on living alone either. It's overrated. You know what your name, Silka, means, right?"

"I thought it meant silky like the fabric or a luxurious feel," she said.

"Well, it might, but there is a very definite meaning to your name in Aramaic. Silka actually has two definitions. It means beets, as in the vegetable, and it means the one who deprives his, or in your case her, adversaries of beets, meaning Silka is the one who conquers her opponents."

"Were beets that important back then?"

"I suppose so."

"How did you know this?" she asked.

"I know things—usually. Not always. My knowledge is completely fallible. But if I have a question, I can frequently receive an answer."

We had finished dinner mostly. Silka picked at a few of the remaining vegetables in the pot, mostly carrots and potatoes, from our standing position leaning over the sink. There was not a single chair or table in my apartment so we ate our dinner in the kitchen. It took me back to my younger days when I did not own a thing, not as now when the items in my former home would possibly be held for ransom by my aberrant spouse. "I was wondering if we could do something," I said. It had the ring of a double entendre as I heard myself speak the words, so I quickly added, "would you go with me to my old house so I can get some of my things? I'm afraid there will be some nasty dealing by my wife otherwise. She might hit her head on the wall and call the police on me. Or give herself a black eye on an edge of the counter."

"Yeah, I guess so. She's not going to attack me, is she? She's not some crazed animal, is she?"

"No, not with me there. Can we take separate cars? I can get more of my junk that way. I hope she has not sold my paintings."

"Sure, I'll follow you," Silka said.

Silka and I walked out to our cars in the chill night after dinner. The temperature had dropped from earlier in the day to about forty degrees. Since I was unsure how well she knew the city, I decided it was best for me to catch all the green lights, so she wouldn't get lost trailing after me and perhaps not be able to find her way back home again. It always took a little concentration and effort on my part, but except for a few major intersections across the city, I was able to switch the lights here and there and up ahead, as I drove, from red to green, and I could do it at will. Many strangers and acquaintances that had ridden in my car found this gift of mine remarkable, but more often than not I played dumb or as though I was confused by what they said, when they commented that I had hit five or six or however many green lights in a row. It was a game I played, acting dumb. A dumb person or one who is perceived to be dumb can fly under the radar more easily. Once later in my relationship with Silka in the car coming back from Daytona Beach, about an hour's drive, and upon approaching our apartments from the outskirts of Orlando, I had hit twenty-two green lights in a row. Silka, it turns out, was a big fan of the ocean during winter, as I have always been. It is much less the tourist trap then I find.

My friends during college had loved to ride with me because of this knack of mine with traffic lights and that I drove a comfortable, large, old Mercedes Benz. We could exit our sleepy college town in no time and be amid the green rolling hills of the Iowa countryside in a smooth and usually much needed transition. And if we headed for a destination in Des Moines by chance, usually a rock concert or a sporting event, I could get us there with relative ease though none of us knew the city well. Thirty years later I can still navigate unknown streets and come out where I should be, when I should be.

We rolled down the broken driveway of our apartment building, the rain-bleached concrete protruding slightly at jagged angles here and there on both sides of the drive with a well-defined fissured slump in the middle. It reminded me of the formation of the earth complete with plate tectonics, pushing the mountains up and scoring the valleys from the tumultuous activity of precipitation and volcanoes. I could imagine universes within universes or at least a host of earths within a single globe. I saw all the microcosms in one and knew why they were there and how they functioned.

I pulled out onto the street and hung a left at the stop sign. It was about nine o'clock in the evening, and traffic was lighter than normal, as it usually errs to the frantic side in Orlando. Orlando, like most Florida cities, has sprawled over decades without any true pattern or logic to its growth. There are areas of nice homes and smart-looking businesses and just down the road one can view shanties and industrial lots with chain link fences and tar strips covering beaten paths.

I flicked on the radio as I drove along. It put me in a state of repose, and I was better able to navigate the mean streets, accelerating and decelerating to go right through the greens. I was playing a smooth jazz station, the kind of music I did not have to pay attention to or worry about, and that would likely be muzak at a premature juncture in its life. The song was interrupted near the end and I could readily distinguish Silka's voice over my car radio. At least it was her voice I thought I heard. I wondered if a time warp had occurred, as radio waves do strange things sometimes, bending back on themselves rather than shooting straight out into the heavens, and when this occurs they are often harbingers of bizarre tidings.

I heard a kind of prewar 1930s radio program, an old style melodrama, the type with those interesting sound effects. The hero's motivation in these shows was usually something like he needed money for his mom's operation and had just lost his job, or he had to figure out a way to keep his kid brother, who had been framed by unscrupulous mobsters, from going to jail. The radio program was set in the '30s it seemed, with that style of speech and expression and idiomatic language of the time, including the unmistakable clanging of sheet metal to represent thunder and creaking doors, as if a stately manor were haunted and foul play was afoot. But the show had a distinctively and oddly modern flavor to it. The narrator had that rich, deep baritone radio voice of the '30s, a facsimile of which was so often heard in those insipid public service announcements later in the postwar era, which sounded naïve and condescending at the same time.

The star of the show a woman with a sultry voice said, with comments from the narrator interjected… "No, I can't lend you any more money… 'our heroine said' …What did you do with the two hundred I just gave you to pay your rent?"

It seemed as though the action on the airwaves was in the form of a play, which might have been commonly heard in the 1930s or '40s, as I have made note.

The narrator bellowed in that familiar sounding tone, which was immediately followed by a male actor's voice, "looking sheepish, her unlucky lover said… 'I needed to pay off a debt, Sylvia. A gambling debt. The mob was looking for me. They were going to kill me.'"

"You bought drugs, didn't you Clive? Don't lie to me. I thought you kicked the smack habit. You promised me, Clive, you wouldn't shoot up again."

"Sylvia, it's not what you think… 'the forlorn man answered' …I just needed to…"

The signal faded out. It then sounded like static from a cheap battery-operated radio on a cloudy night, not the expensive CD changer and satellite radio that came with my Caddie. I'll never quite know what father's fascination was with the radio. I was not fooled one bit. He found the invention quaint and useful I guess and a good way to screw with someone's head. But he was possibly demonstrating something for me, or reenacting a scene, albeit with his characteristic flair and his own sense of drama, but perhaps he was unveiling a side of my new friend in her car behind me that I was as yet unaware of. I turned off the radio as we were almost at my old abode. I had caught every green light. I wondered if Silka noticed.

Chapter Three

Silka and I pulled into my former place of residence. She arrived just behind me. I knew she would be fine and that I was not taking her into the lion's den. She would not become a sacrifice if I had anything to say about it; in fact, I was beginning to believe that if I saved her somehow, she would return the favor. How these details worked out exactly I had no clue.

I had been immediately drawn to Silka. The very strong sensation between us felt right. Energy and one's place or moment in the physical landscape, some would call it chemistry and timing, I guess, but it goes way beyond ordinary garden variety chemicals and the numbers on a clock or the season of one's life, worked to our advantage. Silka was new to Orlando and I had lived in the city most of my life, and it probably had to be so for us to feel an initial connection and need. I was generally not well-regarded in my city—as an artist, somewhat, but not as a person—though this injurious reputation was largely unearned on my part, and Silka knew nothing of my infamous repute and was thus free to form her own opinion. Furthermore, she knew almost no one who could inform her otherwise than that I was a solid stand-up member of my community, which I actually am. But I knew my day of reckoning was coming and I had to establish a bond with someone that could help me, or I would suffer a most ignominious fate.

One of the first things I noticed about Silka that evening in the coffee shop and again in my apartment soon after was that she had a delicious scent that surrounded her, an enticing, magnetic aroma, one of unbridled passion that looked, even begged for someone to sheppard or channel it. I could detect her rather obvious pheromones and though she was mostly unaware, I think, of the effect she had on the male of her species, the result was not something lost on me. Chemistry was not the root cause of my attraction, however. It is not so difficult, as many believe, to come by ardent chemistry. The body and mind can be easily fooled into accepting and promulgating chemical reactions in some heated cause, which really might be tepid to start.

Chemicals can be manufactured, even if they arise internally and are not synthetic; there is a way to speed or aid in their rapid production as well, especially pheromones. Scent is a powerful weapon. A man will remember what aroma a woman gave off years after the dissolution of the relationship. Meditation has helped me in this regard as have olfactory hallucinations, which I am prone to. But being in the exact moment is a far trickier thing, I find, and it has more to do with the proper dimension of space and remaining in the proper dimension when it comes to affairs of the heart. Silka and I had already begun to share each others' thoughts. I did not yet fully understand if she knew that. One of us would think something and the other would say it. It had not yet reached the heights of telepathy for which I am famous among certain previous girlfriends, but our bonds of emotional involvement and responsiveness were clearly developing.

So many loving couples become disaffected because one of the members exits the elemental plane they both inhabited when their passion first stirred for each other. This is not necessarily a bad thing—to pass through another door or gateway—but then typically the dissatisfied member, he or she, simply becomes lost and maybe does not deliberately stray and is not perhaps discontented to begin with, but never finds his or her way back to the same element and the same reality in that dimension. And that can be a good thing as well, but too often one will blame the other for how he or she feels.

It is like a rerun on television during which one of the characters of the program does something differently than before that was not part of the original show. A glitch occurs. Illusion, myth, reality are shattered and give rise to questions that have no answer in this space and time. My father can work brilliantly in this case if he has a mind to. Illusion and temptation are his favorite deceptions. He is indifferent more often than not, but when he does take an interest, and it is always a self-serving interest, it is usually at the price of those involved. He hates to see a happily married couple or any happy couple for that matter. It reminds him of what he never had. My father did remarry for a time, but I guess that was ultimately an unhappy union too. He murdered his second wife.

As a result of the couple living on dissimilar planes, the fires of romance gradually diminish and extinguish, communication hits a brick wall, and one or both parties may wander intellectually, emotionally or physically. Sexual dalliances are by no means a bad thing in a committed relationship necessarily; they often strengthen and encourage connections, but at some point the couple must meet and be together, not as a role of one of inevitability or in a self-effacing manner for either, but together at least. Frequently, couples cannot even live together successfully and this is only part of being a pair. I know about pairs and twins: I have learned my lesson about twins.

I am not one to preach, obviously, as I sit in my car, dreading to even get out of my vehicle and enter my old homestead where my wife of nine years lies within, whom I must inform of our impending divorce. She had a lot of power over me and had turned very sadistic.

Unfortunately, it is so easy to get lost and grow unhappy and blame others for our misfortune, when really the source of hard luck often does not stem from the other person. And I suppose most of us never quite have that feeling of wanting a true union, and I do not feel bad, or pity them. A union is a tremendous and joyous burden and to be so bound, I believe, is a special feeling, in a special moment, and very rare, arduous and fleeting. I felt this for the briefest of times with my wife. My obligation to her, however, became one of duty. And I had to question if duty was enough to sustain me—apparently not.

I took a deep breath. Silka may not be entering the tangled predator's web, and even though we entered the same place in the same dimension and time, it was probably for me the most toxic environment I could issue forth into. Like a cat that sees something, or with felines more likely, that they feel something in the night, my hair was raised and every follicle of my being stood at attention. Silka more likely would not feel this, or perhaps she would. Perhaps she would understand my discomfort. Perhaps she could even assuage my suffering. I would give up a lot for someone who could at least ease my pain. Even a temporary respite would be welcome.

I did not expect a pitched fight exactly. My wife would be surprised that I had gotten out alive, and I would catch her off guard and have the immediate upper hand, and I had a fellow combatant at my side, but something ugly was about to happen. I wondered what she thought of Snooker's missing. She must be aware then I was still alive, I considered. It would be ugly what waited inside. With me those ugly incidents concern loss. I had a brother once. I lost him at an early age. He was father's favorite and when he died father turned his back on his wife of twenty-six years and his two remaining children. Duty was not enough to sustain him either. My younger sister, Dinah, and I were left to fend for ourselves. She was not as lucky as I was. She developed a heroin addiction in her teen years and could never shake it. I'm not sure she even tried to get clean. She was basically a lost soul and lost to her surviving brother, though we keep infrequent contact.

I knew as well it was likely this ugly episode, whatever it was that would transpire inside the walls of my former abode, that the worst of it would happen to me. I knew also that I was never coming back here to live. The final shoe had dropped on my marriage and I was actually glad that it had. It had been a long time coming. I had to get my things, as many of them as I could for now, of which my paintings and the contents of my safe were most important, and get out and make a clean getaway and never return. I would sacrifice my other personal effects if need be. The air in my house would be like poison. I half-expected the door to creak in sinister fashion and bats to fly out of the chimney. I expected hands that I could not see grab for my throat. And there was always that familiar foul stench. There might as well have been a rotting corpse under the floorboards.

My wife had a long history of being abusive, one she perpetuated on others at every chance, and one she particularly enjoyed sharing with me, her legacy to me. It had been a fairly risky proposition for me to close my eyes at night with my wife in the house. I had taken another bedroom just a few short years into our marriage and installed a sturdy locking clasp to ward off those unpleasant surprises in the middle of the night, like being awoken to an ax or a gun in the vicinity of my face. A dagger to the neck is a most inhospitable form to wake up to.

As it was, before we found separate sleeping accommodations, my prospective ex-wife liked to squeeze my nostrils together in the middle of the night so I would wake up gasping and out of breath. She knew I could not easily return to sleep. She, of course, always feigned sleep, but I knew physical manifestations of the spirits in such a manner were rare, so I was always left to conclude my snoring had disturbed her. She could not sleep, so neither would I be allowed to. But then I understood this behavior entirely. Anger, rage, malicious acts—contrivances such as these ran rampant in my family for as long as I can remember.

I had grown up in a very vengeful family. Oddly, my mother was the more merciless of my parents though she would lend assistance often, if I had a true need and was able to convince her that there was something drastically wrong in my life. If she could help, she would, but she was not an entirely capable person. She was competent intellectually and mentally, for the most part, until some point in her life, but that is not the same as being a capable, able person who can get things done, solve problems in a reasonable fashion and help others with theirs.

My father's abuse was more capricious; his dealt more with whim or fancy, while my mother's was very purposeful and more engaged with achieving a certain result, but hardly ever produced the results she intended. Her form of love and care, therefore, which could be discounted or sloughed off like dandruff, was not necessarily the more cruel and punishing, as it was the more ineffective in regard to my father's. My father tended to play his tricks and he was very spiteful on occasion, and always exacted his price with or without due reason. I would say as well my mother, Edna, was paranoid and delusional often, and out to get anyone that caused her or whom she thought had caused her the slightest bit of discomfort. Nevertheless, she was very law abiding, so her relentless pursuit of tearing someone down came in the form of destroying reputations, whispers behind someone's back and malicious slanders for which there would be no easy recourse sought against her. Reputations are deeply personal possessions that don't easily correct themselves or heal on their own. With her children, Edna took practice in reinforcing and strengthening negative and inappropriate behavior. And both my parents had huge egos: that pesky item was an obvious flaw in them both.

When I married Alison, I had essentially married my mother, which is common for some men in their first marriages. My mom was a familiar demon, the devil you know as the saying goes; she was a demon I knew and understood, and one I had actually lived with successfully until I was about twenty-five, after my first disastrous foray into college, and my return to Orlando with my tail between my legs. I was at that point unable to get out of her house. I was ill and decrepit and had attempted suicide while away at school. I needed to stretch my legs, relax and breathe and find some point of reference in my life that I had lost. Several years went by.

My father was the chief manipulator of my first miserable failure in college, based solely upon the fact that I disagreed with his choice of colleges for me. Defying my father always brought the pain. He wanted me to go to a large state school in Florida, where of course, the tuition was much less expensive though he had millions, but I followed the money trail after all, a full scholarship to a small private college in Iowa.

I knew what I would face in college. But I also knew I had to go. I had told Mademoiselle Blancheflor, my third year high school French teacher, the difficulties that lay ahead for me in college, and she had begged me not to go at first. But my reasons for going were clear to her. There is great opportunity in calamity, personal and otherwise, and it has always been so, and I expected to find reward in mine.

I got out of my car and walked toward Silka. I opened her car door.

"You ready to do this?"

"What exactly am I doing?"

"Moral support," I said. "You're keeping my wife from another attempted murder, and keeping her or possibly me out of prison."

We walked up the stone path—I had laid the rock with my very own hands—and we climbed the three steps to the front porch and I unlocked the dead bolt on the front door and stepped into my spacious great room with Silka close on my heels. She did not seem timid as a mouse, more curious and interested in how I had lived with my wife. I could tell Silka was an inquisitive one. I respect curiosity. There would not be so many obvious clues as to my past life of matrimony. The great room, with the river view and the hardwood floors, seemed much larger than it had and the pine floor was unobstructed with clutter; there was no untidiness and disorder of the teak furniture and Chinese silk rugs that had once lain upon it. I took another deep breath.

"I see you decorated your house like your apartment," Silka said. She was referring to the rather obvious lack of furniture in the living room and throughout the entire house. Everything had been stripped bare to gaping holes where the light socket coverings had been and even the cable television switch plates were gone, all taken from the home, and the rooms were barren and empty, except for my paintings, which rested undisturbed on the walls. I guessed I was about to hear yet another interesting yarn from my wife. I wondered how shot through with lies this account was going to be.

As my wife entered from the kitchen, her eyes grew large, round and white upon seeing me walk through the door, but in characteristic fashion, she did not flinch, nor did she miss a single beat, and started in immediately with the interrogation. She always tried to play offense, but I knew I had the ball in my court, and I was about to zip it past her so quickly she would not see a thing coming.

"Who is this?" Alison asked. Her tone signified a demand, a confrontation, a slur to one's manhood and an open invitation to brawl, as it always was with her.

"A friend that you need not be concerned with. I filed for a divorce today."

"Fine. You can have it."

"Where's all our stuff?" I asked.

"We were robbed. Can't you tell?"

"Robbed by the highest bidder?"

"No, just robbed, asshole," my wife said.

"I would temper my tongue if I were you, Alison. The Danish police are still looking for you. It is not so difficult a matter to have a suspected felon extradited as you might think. I am sure my father knows someone."

"I don't know who you are, but run like hell, missy, while you still have the chance" my wife said to Silka.

"We'll see," Silka said. "I have a lot of brothers. He doesn't scare me."

"You're a fool and an idiot," Alison said.

"She's even more pleasant in the morning," I said to Silka. "Dear," again I was speaking to Silka, "can we load my paintings into our cars, please? Here are my keys. I'll be right back." I went to check on the contents of my safe. The safe was bolted to the floor and I had a feeling nothing was missing. I had bought it with hurricanes, thieves and fires in mind. Naturally, I never gave Alison the combination.

Alison followed me into the third bedroom. "So how did you get out?"

"It's quite funny actually. You'll enjoy this," I said, feigning a cordial tone. "I managed to shut off the gas you left on. And one of the bolts was missing on the radiator, so I jimmied it back and forth with my knee and my elbow and eventually popped one side of the radiator loose from the floor, and then slipped the handcuffs over. Of course, I couldn't exactly get on a flight home with handcuffs on, so I caught a cab to the nearest police station." I rather enjoyed telling the story of my great escape. I could tell how insignificant it made Alison feel.

"The cabbie liked the fact that I could speak Danish and the ride was just a few blocks, so there was little charge. I had coins in my pants. The Danish police know all about you. I wouldn't fancy Copenhagen for another vacation, Alison. They also knew they were not Danish policeman's issue handcuffs, so they believed me when I told them it was a lover's spat, which was sort of true, and a fine lad cut the hardware right off of me. It took a little fancy talking from me. I don't know how much time in a Danish prison cell you would get for stealing my wallet in addition to attempted murder. You forgot to take my clothes and passport, luckily. The missing wallet complicated matters a bit. May I have it back?" I spoke politely, but my wife knew I meant business.

"The robbers stole it. It was on the kitchen table. How did you get a flight with no money? I cashed in your ticket."

"American Express lives up nicely to its reputation. I got money orders and a flight within twenty-four hours. They even delivered the money orders to my hotel room."

"How did you get a hotel with no money?"

"American Express. It was a simple matter. I made a long distance call and gave customer service my social security number. It was a lovely room unlike that hovel of an apartment you took me to in hopes of murdering me. Now I have to decide what I am going to do with you. Prison is too easy." I was bluffing, of course. I had no mind to punish my wife; I just wanted her out of my life, and as the final straw had snapped, I could now move on. I did hope I could have her looking over her shoulder for a time. She knew I was quite unpredictable, so she might remain off guard for some time or obsess over what I might do to her. I know from my mother and father's divorce what a bumpy, disagreeable ride a divorce can be, and any advantage can be a welcome one.

"Empty your safe and get out. And take miss flava of the week with you. How long do you think dating your daughter is going to last?"

"Well, let's see…dating a whore like you lasted nine years. I see a future for the two of us. Maybe we'll get hitched and have a kid or two if things go well."

"Get out."

"Darling," I said to Silka as I reentered the living room; Silka had fortunately for me finished loading the rest of my artwork into our cars, so I continued my train of thought and said, "it's time we left the mean old witch to her own devices. There are probably some small animals in the neighborhood she wants to torture."

"Right behind you, Chris," Silka said. Upon exiting the house and extending beyond my wife's earshot, Silka said, "nice woman."

"Tell me about it. Nine years I was married to her. Nine years of my life I spent with her. I apologize for having you meet her, but it was the only way. You handled yourself wonderfully. And you must know, Silka, whatever transpires between us, I will never harm you. It's not in my makeup."

We had gotten to our cars, and I closed Silka's car door for her so she could follow me back to our luxurious apartment building. At least I felt safe there. I doubted that I would get a decent night's sleep in my apartment, but it was now more likely after facing my wife and getting out with my skin intact. I wondered if Silka would agree to help me decorate my new dwelling, or if she enjoyed such matters, seeing as how I was left with nothing in the way of personal articles or effects.

I guessed my ugly scene with my wife was over for now. If I was lucky, I might never have to see her again. I would likely never see my things again. I could buy a bed and a nightstand and a few such sundries. Most of my possessions were lost for good, I was fairly certain, but then maybe it was time to let them go. I could make a clean break and a clean start. I had my gun, forty thousand in one-hundred-dollar bills, my passport, which was in my apartment, and a half-dozen nearly flawless diamonds, first cut and nearly a carat and a half each, which I had recovered from my safe. Silka had inadvertently distracted my wife at just the right moment as I emptied the contents of my safe. My wife did not see what I put in my bag, not that any of it was hers, but she would likely have tried to stake a claim if she had known. She believed the contents to be papers and such. Silka's timing was good I could tell. It might work in conjunction with mine. There are no accidents or coincidences on earth.

I wondered though if my wife had resided over an estate sale and disposed of everything that way. She knew she could get more for my paintings from an art dealer, so she would not have been inclined to sell them to attendees of a garage sale. If that was the case and she did sell everything, she might be planning a move out of town; out of state would be even better. I could only hope.

I was not as fortunate with the traffic signals on our return home, and Silka kept good time with me again as I forged our path ahead. I was finding her very levelheaded and calm. My wife had a pernicious air of danger about her, but Silka was largely unaffected. My wife's energy almost choked me. Silka and I pulled up to our parking spots, side by side, and I opened her car door and said, "I have an idea."

"And what might that be?" Silka asked.

"Why don't we unload these things, and I can help you with them this time. Thanks for getting them in our cars by the way. How about if I take us to a fancy nightclub? There's the Roxy on Bennet Road and Destiny probably has a live band. They're both kind of fun places. I don't get out much, so it should be a fun time. I feel a little like a celebration. We can have a drink or two, talk a bit more and I'll drive. And you can relax."

"Sounds good. I can dance. It will be my first night out in awhile too."

"Oh, you're a dancer. This just gets better and better," I said.

"Do you dance?"

"No, I'm the worst, but I love it when gals can dance. It's sexy." My eyes were eager to attend her every movement on the dance floor, and I was excited by the prospect of seeing my newest friend shake her body in bold rhythms. I hoped she was a good dancer.

"I need a shower and about thirty minutes. Is that okay?" Silka asked.

"Yeah, sure. Take the time you need. The night is young. I don't usually look forward to sleep. I can hang my paintings, if I have nails and a hammer in my trunk."

"I've got nails and a hammer in my apartment. Let's put your work in your apartment and I'll get them."

We dropped off my work and I went up to Silka's third-floor apartment and got her hammer and about two dozen nails. Her apartment was splashy with lots of color on the walls, especially greens and yellows, which she obviously had painted herself, and modern-looking furniture with a large black lacquer armoire, to which the doors were wide open, displaying a nicely sized television, and Silka had laying all around the floor in front of it pillows of various sizes and hues. She rummaged through a yellow and black toolbox with the name DeWALT brazened across it, which rested in her broom closet off the hallway and produced the hardware I needed.

"Nice apartment," I said.

"Thanks. A few of my mom's things. It was kind of a shock when she passed. It was six months after dad died. I had never been to a shopping mall before, when they were alive. I bought the pillows at one. Can you believe that?"

"Yes, I can. You had everything you needed. A big family, a farm. You can't buy those things. Well, I guess you could buy a farm."

"If you can afford one. The price of farms is sky-high. I could never afford one again, I believe. But I don't think I would ever go back to farming again. It's a tough life.

I'll come up in about thirty minutes. You're going to hang your work, right? I want to see what it looks like in your apartment. "

"Sure, we can have a grand unveiling. Time to wake up my neighbors. Thirty minutes." I walked downstairs to hang my paintings, but a small voice inside me said there was no need at present, so I heeded its advice and instead I opened the locking wood case with the black velvet interior, which held my diamonds. Diamonds are the most fascinating minerals on earth, not solely because of their value, but rather they house universe upon universe inside them, and take essentially an eternity to develop and are then frozen in stasis for another eternity. Several of mine were Belgium first cut stones, the cutters in Belgium being far ahead of their trade at one time and having as a result an ample supply of superior gems. I could stare into the precious stones for hours.

There was a knock at the door.

Chapter Four

Silka stood before me in her splendid nightclub couture, a streaming black skirt cut just above the knee and black leather boots, knee-high, with three-inch heels and rounded toes, and a sheer top of black and white that crisscrossed her breasts, revealing just a hint of an enticing but not overpowering femininity. Her blondee hair flowed generously around her shoulders, and standing at my door as she was—she was almost six feet in stature in her boots. She wore a modest suggestion of blue eyeliner that graced her large green eyes as her pearly teeth sparkled against her glowing slender face and red lips. Her chin was soft and round and poking through her shirt her exquisite neck appeared sinewy and strong. Her body looked fun and inviting and I wished this was a second or third date.

We walked down the remaining flights of stairs, with my arm slipped around her thin waist, and out to my car. I opened the door for her.

"How do we get to the Roxy?" Silka asked.

"We'll go south to East Altamonte Drive to 50 West to Bennet Road." I expected Silka did not have her bearings yet, and as there always seemed a fair bit to do in Orlando, she would enjoy knowing her way around better.

"What else here is fun?"

"Well, I like Lake Apopka over by Winter Garden. And then there are the tourist things. Disney is south of us near Lake Buena Vista, and there's International Drive, of course. Universal Studios is on Universal Blvd, which is off International Drive."

"Do you like the tourist attractions?"

"I did when I was a kid. The traffic is crazy on International Drive now. I avoid it like the plague. I avoid I-4 at all costs too. It's always backed up with an accident. I was nine I think when Disney World opened up. My mother used to like to take me there," I said. "We had some good times there. She loved to get lunch at the Contemporary Hotel and point out the very artistic frescoes and friezes. We couldn't afford to enter the theme park most times, and the prices have skyrocketed since then, so we would just get lunch at the Contemporary, which was not too expensive, and not go on any of the rides. We would not even go in the Magic Kingdom; instead, we would take the monorail straight to the hotel and then the parking lot. It was fun. Parking was free, perhaps, it still is. Those were fun times. Lean, but fun times. I don't know quite how my mother afforded my private high school. It is very expensive now. She was a master with the monthly budget till she became ill, but she's doing okay now, I guess."

"I'd like to meet your mom. You know, at some point. I'm not trying to rush things. I don't want to push, but I like meeting a person's family. It says a lot about the man."

"Well, you can if you want. I'll take us there. If you're sure. She's in a mental institution."

"Oh," Silka said and then was silent for the rest of the drive to the Roxy.

I wondered if it was too soon to tell her what I just had. My father had put my mother there somehow, he and his scurrilous, indecent practices and hideous disabling tactics of mind abuse. Insanity did not run in my family, at least not on my mother's side. I don't know about my father's; he was always hush-hush about his parents. My mom was forcibly presented with matters designed to drive her insane, and I suppose my father was successful. He usually was. I am fairly certain it was he, but I could never prove anything or entirely convince myself it was so. There is always some measure of reasonable doubt where my father is concerned. Now she is much older so the dementia seems more natural in a way.

My mother led a wholesome, well-cared-for life growing up on the farm though her mother had died in childbirth giving birth to my mother. That always leaves an unalterable and damning scar, which can never be fully forgotten. My mother was barely saved during her birth, but a clever country doctor was able to get air into her lungs in a sufficient amount of time. My mother never cried, the doctor had stated, or so the story goes. It was as if she knew her journey ahead would be a difficult one and she refused to shed a tear. I only saw my mother cry once; the occasion was the death of my older brother. That was in large part due to my father as well. He, my older brother, was both their favorite.

To hear my father tell the tale of his side of the family, which he would do only if pressed for details, the members all died when he was young. His father died in a boating accident when my father was ten, and his mother died in a car accident when my father was thirteen. Both accidents had always sounded suspicious to me, particularly his mother's, as there was not a lot of automobile traffic at that time, but she could have hit a tree, I suppose. The story changed every time I asked about it, so I finally quit asking.

My father always said he raised himself like a lone, abandoned wolf cub sucking at the teat of a nursing dog for sustenance. He hustled drugs and numbers for the mob as a young teen, slept outside on heating grates in snowy winters and ate at soup kitchens twice a day. Sometimes he would have to catch a bus across town, if he had the change, or walk fifteen miles in the slush and ice, so he could go to a different soup kitchen if the workers of the one he usually attended became wary of his presence or the kitchen was overrun by social worker types or city employees, which occurred infrequently, but on occasion.

He would always join some destitute family with a little boy or girl in tow, concealing himself in this manner, so it would look like they were the members of his family that he was eating alongside of. No one usually asked too many questions, but it was a rough and tumble environment, not one for a lad in transition from a boy to a man. He grew up quickly, engaging in lots of street brawls—had his first knife fight at age fifteen—and had many early sexual encounters, and he learned to take care of himself and steal what he needed and not get caught. A piece of fruit here, a picked pocket there—he was a rogue gypsy child roaming the streets of New York, ducking the police at every opportunity.

We pulled up in the Roxy parking lot. I opened Silka's door. She flashed a brilliant patch of her right thigh as she climbed out of the car, which left me with longing and hope for the right moment. The parking lot was crowded, though it was a Thursday night, and the time was around eleven pm. After a shower and moving my paintings into my apartment, the festivities, I imagined and hoped, should be in full swing at the club. I paid the twenty dollars at the door for Silka and me, and upon stepping through the metal door I could feel the vibrations of electro house music wash over me. I was immediately uncomfortable and had a feeling of impending disappointment, as an ominous mood suddenly came over me, not exactly one of doom or annihilation, but a sensation that made me understand that this evening would not go as planned. I had no particular plan for the evening, but the night would go awry somehow, I was certain.

The organ and synthesizer club music with its pounding unrelenting drum beats hurt my sensitive ears. I had not been to a nightclub in some time, and I swiftly remembered why, but I still felt it might be a good distraction for Silka: a night of dancing, a couple of drinks, and some limited conversation as the music was really quite loud. I did not find it deafening, but close. Silka and I were lucky and found a suitable table in the back of one room and I ordered a Heineken for myself and she indicated she would like a Cosmopolitan. The service was excellent I noted; the evening's theme was models and bottles and the regular club DJ was servicing his audience. Buxom models with a pleasant attitude and kind smiles, always mindful of who might be a good tipper, waited on Silka and me, and it was not long before a young, handsome man, much closer to Silka's age than I, boldly strode up to our table and asked her to dance. I guess he did not count me as a likely candidate for Silka's boyfriend or lover, rather a co-worker he probably thought or a friend or such.

"Should I?" Silka asked me.

"You said you wanted to. Go ahead and dance with him. I'm not the insanely jealous type. And there are plenty of bouncers if there's a problem. I'll sit here and guard our drinks. I would like to see you dance," I said.

The lithe smooth-skinned Silka stepped out onto the crowded dance floor and gracefully undulated and shifted her airy and petite girth to and fro as she moved rhapsodically to the enchanting, forceful beat. It was quite a treat for my eyes. I had not been with a younger woman since my younger years, and though Silka and I were still in an awkward friend stage, not yet lovers, but more interested in each other than merely passing acquaintants, I imagined what might be mine in a carnal way before too long, if I was lucky, and I grew excited and a little stiff at the notion. As a rule with women, I had been a lucky man until I got married. I did not know if my luck had changed entirely or for the better or the worse. I would have to wait and see.

It was unlikely I would venture onto the floor. Silka had understood this about me. My dancing was not only an embarrassment to me but others as well were painfully aware of how badly I gyrated to sound and vibration when I was brave enough, or more likely drunk enough, to step onto a dance floor. The alcohol never improved matters when it came to my dancing.

At my age of almost fifty, and feeling nearly every bit of it, I simply found it hard to keep up, particularly with young athletic women. Though off the dance floor, I had little worry that my years would be a burden or disappointment for Silka. I was still very vigorous in work and play, as well as a more seasoned lover than most men; I was just slower and less flexible than I had been in my prime physical years and, as a result, a little less graceful and more stumbling. I was not, however, in the habit of needing to apologize after sex.

And the element of fun was still happily there with me, and it abounded and came out around women, in the bedroom, and the kitchen whipping up something delicious for the two of us, late nights watching movies and talking face to face on pillows, and through the travels I found myself engaged in regularly: all things I looked forward to with a young, energetic companion like Silka. I felt confident of my ability to offer this very elusive commodity of fun and entertainment to women of a mind to take the opportunities they were extended. I am not, however, without my high-strung artistic side, moody on frequent occasion, prone to depression and confusion over simple details, but never morose, more contemplative and introverted and sometimes sad and angry. Other times, though rare, I chat incessantly like a cooing dove, and at such time my energy is boundless, and my partner may find the need to extricate herself from my presence or I will go on until the light of day.

I was drinking my beer, taking in the various scenes at nearby tables, when my cell phone rang. I kept it only for emergencies, usually the type of emergency that comes on the road that frequent motorists encounter from time to time. Silka was on the dance floor, and her face and body had started to glisten ever so slightly, and she had barely touched her second Cosmopolitan. It was the owner of the gallery where my paintings for sale were on display, a woman named Chanel Reitz of the Chanel Reitz Galleries, on the other end of the line.

"Bad news," she said.

"Give it to me," I said. Chanel and I were old friends. We communicated a great deal with few words.

"There's been a burglary at the gallery and six of your large oil paintings are gone with about a dozen of my other fine paintings," Chanel said. "They got several of your charcoal sketches too."

"The nude?" I asked.

"Yes, it's gone," my friend and gallery owner said.

"Damn. I liked that piece. How about the one of the bank?"

"Gone. The only thing left of yours is the one of the auto crash. I guess they were not enthralled by the realism or maybe it was too large for them to transport."

"Danse Macabre." I had titled the piece after an Edgar Allen Poe short story. The accident I witnessed was as gruesome as anything Poe wrote. "Any leads on who did this?" I asked.

"No clues on my end. The cops are investigating, but there's little chance they will turn up anything. Pieces as fine as these will go to the high bidder in a secret auction and then rest in someone's home for years, and likely be passed down through the generations before anyone tries to sell them. And then, only then, they might be discovered as stolen works of art, but that chance is remote as well."

"Did you have insurance?"

"Oh yes, of course. I'll come out smelling like a rose. I overvalued all the works taken by at least fifty percent. I have to bake in appreciation into the insured price. But my patrons and artists will be the ones to suffer. Unless possibly you have other pieces you care to share for sale?"

"I might have. They are my private pieces. But I guess I can drop them by."

"Okay, Chris. Thanks. You are such a gift to me. A Godsend. Haha, right? I am leaving for the Madrid Art Show soon, and I'll be gone for about fifteen days, but my new assistant Tatianna should be able to help you. I'll call you when I get back. We'll have lunch. Bye. And thanks."

I puzzled over the burglary. My friend was beyond reproach. She would not have organized such a thing. Her reputation as an art dealer and gallery owner was of paramount importance to her and she had taken a lifetime to cultivate it. She would not risk it with a simple theft of a few dozen paintings. The burglary did not have my father's earmarks either. He had no need of money from a private auction, and he was not routinely the greedy person like some thought, though the sense of high drama would appeal to him, like a jewel thief escaping high tech-wizardry and befuddling police, or his staging a heist of priceless museum heirlooms. I was a little too smalltime for him. But had he wanted to cripple a particular business owner, as this thievery might occasion and might have been the design, then arson was much more to his taste. He really was quite the Philistine when it came to fine art.

I considered this latest incident seemed a random act of a random universe. I preferred a more orderly universe. This one was so messy. The thought of the burglary and the resulting images I received as I reflected upon it threw me into a state of immediate despair, though I knew it would be a passing condition. I was left feeling very alone and somewhat confused.

I had come upon a startling realization a few days previously. It had made me feel very insignificant. I had figured out recently that in this universe I am alone. Yes, Silka is there and my mother and my sister Dinah, and even my soon-to-be ex-wife, but they are not truly in my universe. I am alone in my universe. I simply exist in their universe, not they in mine.

How can that be I wondered? I exist in a parallel universe, all the time shadowing an existence in many other universes, as it is for us all, but I have found that in my universe, where I actually live and breathe, it is occupied by me alone. It was an extremely disconcerting notion to have happened upon this insight late one night. I am alone and I might have always been alone in my solitary universe spinning through space and time, throughout my personal history, which is a long and illustrious account. As upsetting as the idea was, it explained a lot. I knew too that I need someone to believe in me and all that I am, good and bad, or I will remain locked up so to speak in a universe that counted one lone forgotten wolf. I had been exiled I guessed and I was unsure by whom and for what reason.

I had been reminded the day of my revelation of the "Twilight Zone" episode, in which the man freezes time with a special watch in order to rob a bank without there being any witnesses, and then he breaks the watch accidentally, and all humanity is motionless and frozen to him *ad infinitum*. I understood his heartache. If one takes people out of the equation, then there is little need or motivation to do anything. I was afraid upon realizing that what I might do in my later life, I would have the same response of disaster and insanity to the same bitter loneliness I often feel just as this man on the television show had experienced. The feeling I had, though manufactured to some extent, seemed ludicrous in a sense, but that did not make it go away. Just then, Silka, the fancy peacock, strutted back to our table. I was once again in her universe—a partial reprieve at least.

"Did you see me?" she asked.

"I did. You are a marvelous dancer. It is a joy to watch you, but I am afraid, my dear, the hour is getting late and it has been an emotional day for me."

"Awww. I understand. Maybe we can get take-out on the way home?"

"That sounds good. You have a splendid appetite for many things. You should treasure that always. There's Chinese near the apartments. If we leave now, we can catch them. What do you say?"

"Off we go then," Silka said and we headed out to my car. "Do you need help? I can drive," she said. I politely declined the offer, though I was tired, and after seeing Silka was properly situated in the passenger seat, I got in my car and told her about my disheartening news over at the gallery and my stolen paintings. She was aghast but saw instantly and commented as such that our retrieving my paintings from my previous residence was a timely thing to accomplish. My timing in my universe is supreme and apparently it holds well for when I am in the universes of others. I am forever thankful for that much.

The time was just before one in the morning, and the restaurant, which was not authentic Chinese food at all—more of a southern American-Chinese mix, made more palatable for the average American taste bud—was about to close, but I persuaded the owner to stay open for one last order or two and informed him we would carry out our dinner. I could see on the cook's face how hot and exhausted he looked, but he apparently was well into a second or third wind and told the pretty Chinese girl with the small breasts and dumpling-shaped eyes at the register it was okay. He was just about to shut down the gas stoves, but he hadn't quite yet, and as he was going to remain and clean for another hour, so what was one more ticket? I thanked him in Mandarin and informed him he would be seeing me on a regular basis. He was surprised I spoke to him in his native tongue, but Silka was not, as she had not remained in our company; she had returned to my Cadillac to listen to a CD.

I thanked the man again and grabbed our food and proceeded to my car with my evening's lovely companion waiting; the night was winding down and I steered in the direction of our apartment building.

I marveled again at Silka's apartment. It was obvious a woman was queen of the roost, and her abode was not too girlish, though Silka was a youngish lass, but then she clearly possessed her complex, enigmatic woman's side and she seemed already a fitting companion. For her, it did not seem to me like it had to be the proverbial "me, me, me." She perhaps had made it through that stage. We sat on the floor on pillows in front of her coffee table, our legs folded beneath it, and devoured our meal. Fast-food Chinese is better than no Chinese food and the meal was tasty and hot and we had both gone a number of hours since supper, working on empty stomachs as it were and drinking a small, but for me, potent amount of alcohol.

After a proper space of time, I rose up from seated position and announced, "Well, I should be going, I guess." I actually hoped to stay.

"Nonsense. You can sleep on the couch. You don't even have a blanket, do you?"

"No, but I can sleep in my car, I suppose. Aren't those seats comfortable? I've only had that car a couple of months. I had a very successful show in Los Angeles not too long ago."

"They are comfortable sure, but stay here. I'll fix us an omelet in the morning."

"You won't be afraid with a semi-strange man in your apartment?"

"Thrilled more likely. My bedroom door locks. I can probably call 911 and give the dispatcher your name before you can strangle me. I don't see you as the type to risk prison."

"Well, in that case, I shall accept your offer and be very happy for it. I have led a base, mean existence at times, and I will tell you many profound things about me in time, and here's this one: I have never lifted my hand in anger to a woman I am proud to say."

I almost added "or a child" to the end of my sentence, but then I paused and the moment was lost, but I figured Silka would get my point. It sounded stupid to me, and not profound, but I guess I had meant something deeper.

"I'm ready to turn in. See you in the morning," Silka said. And with that she retired to her bedroom and locked her door. She did not cry herself to sleep as before.

Silka awoke first in the morning around seven am, amid the rays of light struggling to filter in through the closed Venetian blinds, illuminating little particles of dust traveling through the cosmos, and she came immediately into her living room. I was asleep in my shorts only, and as it was warm in the tiny apartment, I had kicked my comforter to the floor. Though I lay there unconscious I am relatively certain I could feel Silka's eyes upon me. I have been hunted before, but never by one so lovely as Silka.

I have this habit sometimes of waking up and being instantly awake and fully conscious and completely coherent in the same second I open my eyes, if they were not open as I slept, and it is so even from a deep sleep of several hours or after travels through dreams to distant and strange lands that I am alert and ready to face any challenge like a soldier on the battlefield or a man who is unsure of his company and has one finger on the trigger of his concealed weapon beneath his blanket. I can cock my revolver in my sleep. If a twig snaps or a bird stirs, my honed reflexes will do what needs to be done. Silka saw me open my eyes as she stood there.

"Did I wake you? I'm sorry."

"It's time for me to get up." Before I rose, Silka sat down on the edge of the couch, her soft bottom brushing gently and seductively against my toned midsection. Her touch was electric. I knew what she wanted and had hoped last night it would be so this morning.

"Lie down," I said.

She piled onto the couch next to me, half on top of me, half leaning off my body onto the sofa, and she stroked my hair playfully, looking into my face, as I then rose up bracing slightly on an elbow and pulled her the rest of the way on top of me with my free hand. Her long legs stretched down the couch on top of mine and her feet ended on the couch nearly where mine did. She kissed me. It was our first kiss. She parted her mouth and took in my tongue—the sensation felt smooth and moist and stirred longings in me that had been silent or unattended for some time.

It had been a while for me, married to a wounded and heartless shrew that could only envision my death by summoning harpies to rip apart my soul, but one who I could not force myself to run around on, but then in this moment I was not thinking of my wife. I ran my hand over Silka's back, lean and muscled, and wiggled my other hand inside, between our bodies prone on the couch, and inside her cotton top and felt her superb breasts. They were smooth and natural and she had large nipples. She sat upright and lifted off her top, and lay on top of me again and pressed her breasts into my chest. Then I slid up the couch and under from the weight of Silka on top of me and positioned her sitting upright and ran my tongue over her large nipples and her creamy chest and neck, cupping her yielding and exquisite breasts with my hands.

She stood up from the sofa and told me to lift up the lower half of my body, which I did, and she pulled off my shorts, exposing my manhood to her. I was already stiff and fully erect. She grabbed with her right hand my member and gave it a tight squeeze, and to be so boldly touched by a beautiful woman such as Silka felt as magical as it had any time before. She said, "Get up."

I stood up and she took down her thong and bent her body over the side of the couch, and spread her legs as she faced away from me. I began to rub her swollen clit with my fingers and massaged her sweet spot as my fingers went in and out of her. I squeezed her round ass and bent over her kissing the back of her neck and shoulders. After a brief moment, she writhed a little, moaned, and said a breathless "yes."

I then played with the head of my penis rubbing it over her clit, caressing just the spot that I knew would bring her the most pleasure, until she begged me to enter her and fuck her slowly. I thrust deep inside of her, bringing my cock almost fully out and then thrusting in again, rhythmically and eventually with increasing speed and vigor, and Silka, I knew, could feel the pressure of my swollen penis inside her. The love grew more passionate and I could feel the moist heat of Silka's insides and the heat of the small room.

She began to move her hips from side to side, moaning and sighing, telling me, ordering me, not to stop. I began to thrust more deeply and more quickly for a series of long spellbound moments, and then I could feel her tighten inside against my member, and we came together.

I leaned over her back with my weight holding her tightly to the couch and squeezed her tits and kissed the back of her neck, and I kept my manliness inside her for a moment longer, and then, as if it occurred to us at the exact same point in time, we both laughed happily in simultaneous fashion.

After the passion of our love making, there suddenly came a funny moment between us, and it was a moment we shared—that first moment of sex between a new couple; it was that first moment of the oddity of human sexual relations between a duo, and our laughter gave us light hearts and put us both in a good mood for the rest of the day. We had spent a good deal of energy, the two of us, wondering and figuring out what sex and love making would be like for us, and it had proven to be fun and satisfying, and though the laughter was tinged slightly with relief, it was more so accompanied with the realization that we could perform this act of intimacy together and our rapport could carry forth as lovers. We had demonstrated to each other that the prospect for good relations and a deeper physical and emotional connection between us was possible.

Chapter Five

"Stop it, father. Put me down," I said calmly. My parakeet, Snooker, was squawking up a storm in the next room. My father preferred to strike terror in one's heart, and short of that, he played his tricks and pranks, often nasty ones, particularly when he did not feel well. If one begged him for anything, he was resolute of purpose and would vanquish the unfortunate, misguided soul that labored under the mistaken impression that my father would cooperate. It had always been clear that I could only ask my father for certain things and in certain ways, and if I did so with any voice of an imploring, whiny or yelping pup it was a certain path to destruction.

I had been lying in bed and dreaming of high school, more precisely my third year French teacher and an unpleasant incident in my life. There were actually a series of very unpleasant incidents in high school, and mine were a bit different from most and had greater ramifications longer into my life. I made a bitter enemy in high school, one who haunts me to this day. It was partly my fault and I readily admit this, and given the chance to go back and straighten things out, I would. Perhaps in another universe we are friends, but where my main consciousness is, which is mostly in this universe, we are bitter enemies and he has exacted an awful price from me. His name is Jude and we had started as comrades, sharing many advanced classes together at the academy, but something happened between us and he has vowed ever since that he will get even with me.

The specific point in my past that had crept up on me again dealt with the generosity of my teacher and a certain stupid man, a football coach, who carried a grudge against me. I do not really count this coach as an enemy; he is too stupid to be much of a threat. His was an immature soul that did not understand life. And he did not, this athletic coach, have the power of my nemesis, Jude, that I developed about the same time as a lad while at my prep school, and my foe still tries to suck the blood out of me today.

I did not enjoy high school. I hated it, in fact. I never fit in. College was much better in some ways, but that was a terrific ordeal for me as well. I was the poor kid in high school. As I think I have stated my father had left my mother and me nearly destitute. My sister Dinah was out of the house by my high school years and already lying in a gutter or back alley and needing another fix and wondering how she might get it or what she might have to sell in order to get it. The other students in my college prep academy tolerated me mostly, when a civic bone of compassion or pity rose up in them, and many were quite nice to me and I had some companionship, which when I look back on those years lightens the memory of the burden considerably. My teachers generally enjoyed having me in class, as I was bright and intellectual, but it was a strict, conservative school. Though I excelled in my academics, I was showing signs then of becoming a gifted artist and I was laying the fruits of an unconventional, rebellious and liberal education and personality.

As I lay in my bed and at the time I had cried out to my father, I had begun, with Silka's assistance, to decorate my apartment, and I had purchased a bed and nightstand that met with her standards. My revolver rested on the nightstand next to my bed, and as I did not expect any visitors, I figured it was an adequate place for my gun for the time being. Silka and I did not usually sleep together overnight as yet, and for sexual rapport, we tended to occupy her apartment, as it was more fully furnished and comfortable.

I had been floating in a dreamlike state four feet above my bed, my arms stretched out as on the cross, the covers rippling down around me, a hint of a cool, moist breeze from the winter air and the open window, and suddenly I came crashing down, landing with the most unceremonious wallop on my mattress. I hit my head on the headboard as I dropped, and I could hear laughter in the next room; it was a malicious chortle this time that emanated from the walls and ceiling. I expected my father was looking for a fight. He had not been feeling well lately and could get very nasty if his health was off the slightest bit. I heard too my twins giggling. They thought it quite funny when there was roughhousing afoot, especially if it was me getting roughed up, but their laughter was the laughter of children—innocent, gay and without pretense.

"Very funny," I said when I hit the mattress. Again, I said it calmly, but with greater emphasis. If I had become enraged, it might have turned ugly. My father did not stand for open defiance. There were definite boundaries to respect with him. This world belonged to him for the most part. Mutiny would lead only to a vast struggle and he was much stronger than I, and as we have our differences on many subjects, we kept our distance from one another routinely. He rarely needed me for anything and I only sometimes needed him, so to minimize conflict I would leave him alone as much as possible.

The first couple of times he levitated me it was absolutely terrifying. I learned a few of his tricks though. I could lift a grown man off his feet by clenching his throat tightly with my mind and through extension of my hand, choking him in the process, but never actually touching him. It was not sleight of hand or a magic trick and the unsuspecting never saw it coming. I had tried levitating someone not long after witnessing Darth Vader at his handiwork in *Star Wars*. I had done this to a young man who had pushed me in a high school locker room.

The purpose on my part was to strike fear in a daring opponent if it looked like battle. I have stated I have many detractors. It came in the form of a warning shot across the man's bow. I am older now, and less inclined to wrangle physically, and I never had any true desire to brawl. A few had witnessed my abilities; most had not, but my reputation as a somewhat disagreeable man had traveled widely throughout a number of circles. I don't know how much this attitude toward me reflected reality; I think of myself as a generally helpful, cheerful man from time to time, and certainly not one that looks for trouble. But this rather dangerous standing of mine suited me, as I prefer to be left alone. No one much cared for me, no one much came to my aid, so I felt comfortable in returning the sentiment, when appropriate.

But when I was first the victim of levitation, I thought I was losing my mind. Father found that most amusing, my precarious mental condition, a constant plague from my last years of high school on. The mind was his favorite avenue of attack; it left more permanent and damaging scars than inflictions upon the body. It is more difficult, although this may stand less to reason, for the mind to adapt than the body. This may owe to its greater complexities, which one would think could produce faster and more relevant adaptations, but actually the reverse is true and the process of adaptation for the mind is much more cumbersome and lengthy.

But I was always the superior chess player, the superior strategist. I had to be. I was also more patient than my father. I had to use my wits to outsmart him or I would have been dead long ago. His ire with me was great. How I had survived this long I do not know exactly. I handily took our first ten games of chess in a row from him and gave him the eleventh as a consolation prize, at which he became infuriated. He would never play with me again after that. I had been younger and less respectful of his ego. But we had gotten along better then as I found him more tolerant of me in my youth. His tolerance of me diminished when my older brother died. Father had loved children, even his own once. We were not such a disappointment to him then. I am sure when Dinah first found herself in the presence of a needle that he clandestinely whispered in her ear to give the heroin a try. Temptation is one of the deadliest devices known to mankind.

I glanced at the clock. It was 5:55 am, shortly before daybreak and I lay alone in my bed. I dreamed frequently of late of my third-year high school French teacher, the enticing Mademoiselle Blancheflor, her name meaning white flower, which conjured up images of her brilliance and exquisite virginal qualities. She was an unsullied rose to us, the boys at my academy, picturesque and breathtaking. I felt she might be in trouble and hoped it was not so.

My dream concerned that very ignorant man at my high school, the coach with his ridiculous score to settle, who had planted drugs in a locker, thinking it was my locker he was putting the illicit substances in. Upon spying me in the corridor, he called me over and accused me loudly in the noisy hall so all could hear of my alleged possession of narcotics, and, of course, he claimed I was selling the drugs to my fellow classmates. He was a silly, insignificant man. The coach thumped his meaty index finger against the locker, trying to rally an audience so he could further impugn my character. The dream came back to me in pieces as I lay in my bed nursing my head wounds. I could see the man, balding, sweat on his brow from the Florida heat, his distended belly, those ridiculous polyester shorts, high fashion for a football coach, and his mouth contorted in anger as his tongue flapped uncontrollably. It was quite an embarrassing scene.

"That's not my locker, Coach."

"Go ahead, open it up."

"How am I supposed to open it up, if it's not my locker?"

"You're lying, Devin. Open it up. We found pills and dope in this locker. I think you've been pushing."

"Why should I care what you think? I bet you put the drugs in the locker."

Just then Mademoiselle Blancheflor passed by and said, "He did. I saw him."

"He's trying to get me kicked out of here and I have a full scholarship to college in the fall."

"Don't tell him that," Coach said to my teacher. He was unaware the Mademoiselle and I were on close terms for a teacher and a student. "You're not tenured, you know," he continued.

"You can't threaten me, Coach. You're in no position," my French teacher laughed at him. She then said, "Chris, open up your locker. I'm going to talk to the headmaster about this right now. Now observe, Coach."

I'm glad she had such faith in me that I was telling the truth. I smoked pot as a young man, and on school grounds frequently, quite a number of us did, probably Coach as well, but I was never so bold or so brainless as to leave any in my locker. It would have been too obvious a hiding spot and an immediate excuse for my dismissal from the academy.

"You're the one in possession of street drugs, Coach," I said. I had moxie for a teenager, and I was not intimidated by this strong, athletic man, owing chiefly to the fact that he was so dumb. "And you've falsely planted them in someone's locker and made false witness that they belong to me. That's tampering with evidence, entrapment, slander…I think there are several felonies in there, Coach. And you put them in someone else's locker. How wrong is that?" I could not help but put on a show for my French teacher.

With Mademoiselle Blancheflor looking on, I opened up the locker two over from the one Coach thought was mine and said, "Voila," and laughed at the expression on his crestfallen face. He looked like a sad orangutan. I then took all my pens, notebooks, ties and books out of my locker.

"Just so you know, I am not going to use a locker anymore, Coach. So you can't go planting bogus crap in it."

"This isn't over, Devin."

"Yes it is Coach," the young, lovely Mademoiselle answered, "because you are about to be fired." She had stood by my side before, and this time was no different. She was a petite woman of fine sensibilities with flowing raven curls, and half the size of the livid football coach with the maniacal look in his eye. Mademoiselle had lived in Paris for several years, and she was a grand dame in every sense, though only in her mid-twenties, and she was the object of many a school boy's lustful eye. She had her lovers, I presumed, but was always discreet and her personal affairs never became the subject of much discussion at the conservatory. As my classmates and I tended to speculate about our teachers quite a bit, she, however, remained below our radar, thankfully for her I would guess, though a more handsome woman could not be found on campus.

My teacher and the football coach headed off in the direction of the headmaster's office, and I hustled out to the parking lot with my books and neckties and such to place them in a friend's car. Coach had tried everything he could to get me kicked out. I thought he was going to beat me up once in the men's bathroom. Luckily, he understood force was not the right way to go about this, so he resorted to stealth, but simply did not have the capacity. He reminded me significantly of a tackling dummy.

I was angry, and I thought immediately of telling my mother what had happened, but knew I couldn't. It would have been a useless gesture on my part. She was getting much worse my senior year of high school and drifting in and out of psychosis. I was working a part-time job until midnight about four nights a week, getting up at six a.m. to catch a ride to my high school, which was twenty miles away, cooking for the both of us, doing the cleaning and laundry, spending most days at school until five in the afternoon, and doing homework all night, if I could find time. I took care of the yard and bought groceries, and for about the last six months of my high-school career, I had been in very intense therapy twice a week. The psychiatrist had "comped" me because he knew my father and the rest of my family, and I think he understood that I needed all the help I could get. I received from my psychiatrist, owing to my father's vast influence and suggestions, much more than I bargained for. I was ready to blow my brains out. I had bought a gun. It is the revolver that now rests on my bedside table.

And I was only sixteen, just a child, and barely of legal age to drive a car to a shady spot and spill my blood. I was stuck, and I saw my father's hand everywhere I looked. He hated my choice of college and vowed to ruin the experience for me. He set those wheels in motion before I arrived on campus. And my mother would never tell me what she had seen. It was clearly a vision that had pushed her close to the edge. Perhaps it was some awful premonition. Her malaise had come on her suddenly and inexplicably.

Of course, my father was nowhere in sight, which as I look back was actually fortunate. He would not help me out, angry as he was with me, especially if it meant he might be of some lateral assistance to his ex-wife. Everything fell on my mom's shoulders and she could no longer cope. They bitterly disagreed and fought whenever the occasion dictated, and she never once got the best of him. I was not surprised by that.

I hustled back from the parking lot under the arch and onto the brick patio. The next class I had after the locker incident was French with Mademoiselle Blancheflor. She told me to remain behind after the class had gone. I could barely concentrate during rounds I was so upset.

"Why does Coach want to get you thrown out?"

"It's a very childish matter, Mademoiselle. I told Jimbo to quit the football team because he hates it, and it takes all his time, and he has a girlfriend now and he wants to see her, not see Coach. Jimbo was a good player of Coach's, but he doesn't want to be a football player. Jimbo lives here with his mother, but Jimbo's father sits on the Chicago Board of Trade, and Jimbo wants to go up to Chicago eventually and work with his dad. So Jimbo stood up to him and quit, and Coach is angry with me because I'm an easier target. Then Coach got that promotion, whose clever idea that was I have no clue, so now he thinks he can break me down and get me kicked out of school. And he's planting drugs in students' lockers to do it. What did the Headmaster say?"

"He wanted to speak with Coach first. I had to make an appointment, but rest assured I will talk to him, Chris. This matter will be resolved favorably. You're not in the wrong here. Everything you have said is true, correct?"

"Yes, thank you, Mademoiselle. He's just crazy, and I have a sick mom at home." I was half-glad I finally told someone at my school. I had mentioned it deliberately.

"I didn't know your mom is ill."

"Nobody here knows. She's got cancer, and I still don't know where my dad is and it doesn't matter anyway. He's made it very clear I can't count on him. I'm in therapy now and I don't know how much more I can take."

"Would you like to come over this weekend?"

"To your home?"

"Yes, why not?"

"I can't involve you any more in this situation."

"Why?"

"Because I have feelings for you. Romantic feelings."

"Oh. I see. There are other ways I can help you. Do you think you want to go into someone else's home?

"Foster care? NO! I can't. I graduate in three months and then I leave for college in about six, if I can. I've got a full scholarship, right down to books and a job at a top college. I couldn't go in anyone's home. But I'm not sure I am going to be able to go to college."

"You have to. Your mom will have to find someone to take care of her. Is it terminal? There's hospice, you know. You have a sister in Florida, right?"

Yes, I do, but it's not just that. I lied earlier. I wasn't prepared to say this, but I guess I have to tell someone, and it might as well be you. It's not cancer. My mom has gone...insane."

Mademoiselle Blancheflor had a very disconcerted look on her face.

"And now I'm sick. Do you know what I do for hours after work and on weekends? Sometimes till three or four in the morning?"

"Tell me."

"I stare into my eyes in our bathroom mirror. I swear it feels like fifteen minutes, but when I check the clock, four hours have gone by."

Mademoiselle looked very unsettled after I said that. "You're not well," she said.

"I'm depressed and moody all the time. I can't handle this. I want to kill myself."

Mademoiselle started crying.

"Please don't cry. If I thought I hurt you...I can't take anymore."

She regained her composure.

"You need help. Let me get you in a nice home. I know plenty of families. I deal with exchange students all the time. We can find someone to take care of your mom. You both need help, Christopher."

"No, I can't. I'm the only one that can talk to my mom right now. She's enraged my sister, her former co-workers, the neighbors. She's alone but for me. I can't desert her now. She could do something to herself. And my sister and I don't really get along. No, Mademoiselle please don't tell anyone about this. I've thought about what to do. My doctor is trying to help us. Please don't say anything."

"Okay, on one condition. I'll remain silent about what you have told me as long as you promise me you'll go to college in the fall and take that scholarship. I've seen your sketches. You're very talented. You might be the next Gauguin or Cezanne."

"All right. I promise. I'll go. I swear. I've got to get to Calculus. Prof Harding is going to crucify me if I am late again."

"We'll talk tomorrow. You made a promise."

"Okay, I know," I said and gathered my books and walked out of Mademoiselle's classroom with my head held high. I could not lead on to anyone that I had such a serious problem. I was the odd boy already, and clearly a target for a few, and all I wanted was peace of mind and to be left alone.

Dawn was slowly enveloping the landscape. The night air, which had met its demise for another day, turned dry as daylight seeped in, and the thermometer awoke lazily pushing the mercury into the fifties. It might break seventy today, I thought, as I continued to lie in my bed. The cold snap had snapped.

I needed to stir. I rubbed my head from where I had bumped it, smoothing out the pain in my scalp. Now was an excellent time to paint, before the light of reason whisked away my emotion and crowded into my day. I was pure energy at times like these and I could create with the power of a saint and the gifts of the truly blessed. But it would not last long. Every day was a process of taking away bits and pieces of matter from me, my comfort, my self-esteem, my concentration. And then the night was often horrible, but in those first waking moments, I knew what I was capable of. I went into my latest studio, a makeshift one at best, that I had set up in my apartment. I had been working on a piece inspired by Silka. It was of a large empty room and its harsh, barren walls with a fair damsel standing off to one corner and an older man standing at the opposite end gazing out the window. There apparently was some rift between the couple, but it remained unspoken it seemed and they had retired to separate corners.

I stepped into my second bedroom in my apartment. I immediately detected the odor of linseed oil. My easel sat upright facing away from the solitary window that looked upon the roof of the adjacent building. I studied the room for a moment, mixing my paints, absorbing its energy; the room had a feeling of vibrancy, of raw force to it and something unfinished and yearning for completion, and I could feel the spiritual aspect swirling around the space. I need a window or two in my studio; they are a major source of liveliness and energy and light, and sometimes I paint to classical music, but more often I do not, as I need to concentrate more fully and cannot have my attention diverted even the slightest bit. Snooker now sat high in his cage, resting. Painting is an exacting art, as all the arts are, I guess, but one where the greatest amount of concentration and energy are required. The slightest disturbance and I can lose a day's train of thought and my time becomes wasted.

I began to paint on the homemade canvas, layering the remaining background with colors that would bleed through only partially so I could cover them over and produce the desired the result. I usually work wet-in-wet with bold strokes here and there and more expressive strokes of the brush on figures and objects, and this particular painting had muted colors for the walls and the view outside the room's window, which soften the stark emptiness of the interior space and the sense of loneliness. I had not shown this work to Silka and it was as yet untitled. With luck, I would have it completed in a day or two.

Chapter Six

I was summoned to Florida Hospital in Orlando, Florida. I knew my father had not been doing well, but I did not know the situation was as grim as it was. He lay in a hospital bed, admitted with high blood pressure and some strange disease that had the doctors and nurses baffled, and as there was a team of RNs and physicians working toward a treatment plan, it was clear he was receiving more than adequate medical attention. I have always hated hospitals; I can smell the stench of the dying and the diseased, and my father and I both knew he was not long for this world. He would likely slip into another universe where he was healthy, or figure out a way to be reborn in this one, or possibly both avenues were open to him at precisely the same moment. I did not know for sure. I didn't really care either, but I knew his influence upon this earth and upon me especially was not entirely near an end. He called me to come next to him in the empty, private room.

"It's almost time, buddy boy. I don't suppose you have impregnated any women I don't know about?" my father asked. He always wanted grandchildren and neither Dinah nor I had any kids.

"No, afraid not. What did the doctors say it is?"

"Oh, they don't know anything. I never thought inventing HMOs would bite me in the ass this way. They think it is some type of neuromuscular disease, but they have no clue how to treat it. I'm getting weaker every day and then I guess finally my heart will give out. I hope I'm asleep when it does, but I don't think I'll be that lucky."

"Is there anything you want or need?"

"I do have one final request. I need you to be next to me when I go. Several doors will open up in your mind, and you need to help me pass through the correct one. Can you help your father out, buddy boy? I am not allowed to do it myself and I could be tricked or get confused."

"Yeah, sure. I am sure I can do that."

"That's a boy. I have something to tell you and this might upset you a bit, but then I have prepared to leave everything to you and it is quite an extensive estate as you might imagine, so that might soften the blow that is about to come. You know the psychiatrist in high school that you saw?" my father asked.

"Yeah, sure."

"Well, I paid him a little money to do something that maybe I shouldn't have. I had him hypnotize you. Several times, in fact. I don't know if you remember. He placed several post-hypnotic suggestions in your subconscious. Honest, buddy boy, I was trying to help you out."

My palms grew instantly sweaty and my body was seized with what felt like a high fever. I was scared to ask, but I had to. "What kind of post-hypnotic suggestions?" I asked.

"Well, there were a lot of them actually. To be honest I have forgotten most of them. Things like when you told me how you hate it when people laugh and you are not in on the joke, or it's some kind of inside joke. You said you hated that, right?"

"Yeah, I do. It's always something abusive."

"Well that was one of them. The laughter of children was another trigger. The crying of a woman. When people in discussion interrupt each other. There were quite a number actually, as I recall."

"So what do these triggers, trigger?" I was growing quite uneasy with the direction of this conversation.

"Well, that's where it gets kind of complicated. I think the doc didn't know what he was doing. The suggestions were supposed to evoke strong emotional reactions, but they seemed to have gotten worse with you over time. It also developed into a fragmentation of your personality, and I am not sure that you are aware. But in my defense, you were such a talented painter even then, that I thought if I helped you along, you would develop the greater sensibilities for art that you needed. I readily admit I am not much of an artist, but I know the gifts you exhibited. I always thought you would make a fantastic painter one day, and you have apparently. I'm very proud of the work you have done."

"You never told me you were proud of anything I did," I said. I was growing increasingly uncomfortable and I knew I had to get out of the room, or I might strangle my father right there on his deathbed. My whole life was a lie. It was some trick of hypnotism. A trick of the light. I was not sure who I was or what I was or what was real anymore. "I gotta go," I said abruptly.

"Forgive me, buddy boy. I was trying to help you."

"Like you helped my mother. You can rot in this stinking bed. Shit," I said and walked out of the room, bumping into the doorframe and nearly knocking off some papers that were affixed to the door. *The asshole*, I thought. I lost my bearings and went down the wrong corridor and did not know where the elevator was, but finally located it, and I knew I had to keep my cool and get away from the hospital and my father. I would never murder anyone, but I was not so stupid or naïve as to believe I wouldn't consider it seriously. I had been married a long time. Then it dawned on me. I guessed he had told my wife all of my psychological triggers. She knew every button to push and could do so with ease. *I'll get even with him*, I vowed. *This is not over. That bastard. That asshole.*

I went and sat in my car. I was not going to cry, but at that moment I wished I could have. Instead, my attention was diverted to the developing scene in my head. It did not concern my father, but rather my sworn enemy, Jude, and a woman, whose face I could not see. I could tell she was a shapely woman and she spoke with an accent, but I was unable to distinguish what kind of accent she had. It seemed perhaps Eastern European, but I was unsure, as I heard her speak in my vision only once. The details of the obvious scheme that was being hatched, probably a plot against me, I assumed, were vague and I was already distraught over the news my father had given me so I could not pay full attention. *How dare he have me hypnotized?* And then the scene quickly exited my mind as quickly as it had arrived.

There was definitely some trickery afoot I considered, but the details of the psychic drama were too nondescript and not enough for me to go on, but then I knew more was likely to be revealed to me. I started in the direction of my home. The stock market was open and I needed to sell my natural gas stocks as it was time to take profits and I had a good idea of what to do with some of the money.

As I drove home, I remembered Jude and how we had started out as friends in high school. He and I had taken several advanced classes together. He was brilliant, I always felt, and though my actions against him might have been perceived as jealousy on my part, that was not my motivation. It started as a complete *faux pas* and nothing more, and the improper timing of my ill-chosen words were to my utter shame. I let slip to Mademoiselle Blancheflor that I had witnessed Jude cheating on a Calculus test at an early point during our senior year at the academy. The Mademoiselle had insisted I tell the headmaster. I fought that one religiously, but with the immediate sense of doom that prevailed, I knew I would yield to my French teacher's wishes.

To make matters worse, I had told my mother about the Mademoiselle's insistence upon my doing the right thing, and my mother then also asserted that I tell the headmaster about Jude's academic dishonesty or she would pull me out of high school. And my mother had no reason to care. She was remotely involved at best. Just by being chatty with my lovely French teacher, a woman I respected immensely, I had put myself into a situation that I knew would not bode well for me in the future, and I had no other course of action, and I knew that my dilemma would grow over time. I have been proven correct. But then it was my fault. And Jude has many allies. He seems to pop up often at the same place as I around Orlando, and he seems to know as well as I half the city's population by name, and many individuals are indebted to him, so I feel whenever I am around him or encounter his cronies, I am in hostile territory.

Jude was a terrible womanizer and I believe had turned into an alcoholic, which was not to my chagrin because I felt I had played a role in these circumstances. He was rejected from Washington University, where his entire family had gone to college just about. I assumed the man in the parking lot of my divorce attorney was one of the followers of Jude and keeping tabs on me for some ungodly reason. It did not seem merely like paranoia. The worst-case scenario was he was one of my father's henchmen. I didn't think so though as they mostly drove sports-utility vehicles and I didn't remember seeing one in the lot. They were trouble no matter what so I stayed out of their way.

It had been rumored that Jude had strangled a prostitute and killed her. No charges were ever brought. He had sold three car dealerships that he essentially inherited from his father and made out like a bandit just before running them into the ground, and he had lots of cash and resources and knew key people around Orlando. I barely associated with anyone. I pulled out into traffic and immediately picked up a tail. It was a black SUV. *Shit*, I thought. I slowed down so the man would be forced to go around me, which he did as he chattered away on a cell phone. It was a network they all had and my father was at the pinnacle. It was the beginning of something, but I was not sure just yet what was going on. I had to watch my step in so many ways.

I needed to go home to my apartment. I had told Silka I would take her to a job interview at a fashionable dress company at the new mall, and she did not know the way to get there. I was less angry, and figured my father might have had his reasons why he hypnotized me, at least one or two of which might have operated in my favor, but I was not any more calm than I had been. Something was afoot and I was usually the last to know, and that did not bode well for me quite often. I went up the stairs and knocked on Silka's door. She was ready to go, fashioning stockings, a fabulous green dress cut above the knee that set off her blonde locks and boots. She certainly had a sense of style about her.

"Does it say manager?" she beamed. She saw the approving look I gave her.

"It does," I said, referring to her outfit. "It says Wall Street. It's perfect. We'll get lunch after on me."

"Okay."

We walked out to the car and got in, my assisting Silka with her door and then she attempting to unlock my door as I walked around the back of my car to get in, but my door I had unlocked by remote. It was a gesture I had seen in a movie once. If the woman gets the car door for you, then she's a keeper. Movies have moments if they are good. It was the thought that counted in this case. We motored out to the new mall and I flipped on the radio. It was a continuation of that same circa 1930's-style radio show, the one with the man who was in trouble and the younger lass that saves him somehow or the older man is at least in need of her to save him. I did not know the ending. Silka was deep in meditation about interview questions. I could tell. So I listened to the radio show.

There was a message here for us both, a tacit one, but not of betrayal as I had thought when I listened previously. Now the young heroine was offering to give the man money and she told him if he bought drugs or liquor with it they were through. I had kicked my drug habit years ago and knew thankfully I would never go back to it, and alcohol was not an issue with me. There was something here though and where exactly it was coming from I did not know.

Sometimes radio waves travel a great distance before reaching their intended audience. The show could have been beamed out from the cosmos thousands perhaps hundreds of thousands of years ago. Radio waves that traveled into our sphere here on earth from outside the solar system were once called LGM signals, the LGM standing for little green men. I knew when I heard that in my grade school Physics class that there was some truth to the matter, but how much I was unsure. But that was one reason I was sure there was an important message for me beyond the high drama of modern radio depicting a bygone era. This itch on my brain that I received quite often had happened in a similar manner before and woe unto those who neglect signs from afar. It is always to the detriment of the neglector. I had learned that lesson in life.

I waited in my car while Silka went in for her interview. She said it would be only about thirty minutes and I did not have any need of shopping, so I waited parked in the blazing sun though the day was cool and the air was crisp. As typical, they had laid waste to a huge tract of land and allowed almost no trees to remain standing. There was barely a shade tree left in Orlando. The orange groves were all that lingered and those were all on private property. The city had basically grown to become one vast parking lot.

The summer temperatures run ten to fifteen degrees hotter than previous of just a few years and that was too big a jump in such a short time to be explained by global warming. The simple fact of the matter was that my father was intent on destroying as much of the world as he could, so he could reconstruct one the way he wanted. Earth was his haven and his alone. That is how powerful he was, but he was losing his grip and had begun to die. He might have some other future destination in mind. No one seemed to complain about how weird everything had gotten on earth and there were periods in our history to compare it to that were equally as weird as the present times, so saying this is the only planet we know does not exactly wash. This earth has existed in many different states of being and complexity at many different times. This is a much older rock than most believe. We need only look at ancient technologies like Incan or Aztec or the technology of Egypt to be reminded of this fact.

Earth is the only planet I am aware I have lived on before, but the comparisons of the weird times going on now to the weirdness of before are many and fruitful. One might examine the changes in architecture and its subtle but definable shift to something more gothic and as a result more horrid in these modern times of ours. Banks look like medieval castles with armaments and barred windows, strip malls that are without windows and the retched sight of some apartment buildings that house the unlucky few are everywhere and enough to convince me were being taken back in time. My father might like to stand against the church again in some medieval primetime drama that would affect the life of every resident on earth. In his weakened condition I was not sure he could pull it off. Not just as yet. But we apparently are headed in the direction of returning to some part and parcel of the Middle Ages. He seems to be engineering it that way.

Silka popped out and said, "I think I'll get a second interview for assistant manager."

"Nice. I'm sure you will then." She scooted into my car. "There's a Thai restaurant over here somewhere. I haven't been to it, but heard it's quite good," I said.

"Sounds fine. Let's do it."

I had a confession to make to Silka by now. As we were embroiled in a relationship, I needed to tell her that I am a mentally ill man and I might add it arose from my being raped by a friend of the family when I was ten. He claimed he would rape my sister if I told anyone, so I kept silent about the matter. My father, of course, put the man up to it. I never knew why. I guess I had outlived my boyish attitude and perhaps defied him on some small topic. That was always a mistake that brought me pain. I was not ready to give away to Silka any details of who I really am, so discussion of my father would be kept to a minimum, if at all. Certainly for now it had to be that way. It was not going to be a cheery conversation at first, but the time and place suited me. It was an early point in the day for lunch, and the restaurant had just opened and there were not many patrons. The booths had decorated thatched huts the roofs of which hung down over the tables, making them more private and causing a greater muffling of sound across the restaurant. I picked a booth near a window.

"There's something I must tell you now that we are engaged in a relationship," I said.

"Please don't say you are gay. I already know," Silka said. I was quite startled at the remark.

"What do you mean?" I asked. I said it a bit defensively.

"I'm just kidding. It was a joke. I know you're not gay. You're very ungay, in fact. What did you want to tell me? And now I hope you really aren't going to say you're gay because I'll feel awful now, and so will you if you deceived me."

"No, I'm not gay. I just am in the habit of wearing clean clothes." Silka smiled. I could tell she had heard that one before. It was a lighter moment than I expected, so I launched into my confession. "I have paranoid schizophrenia, Silka, and I do become ill on occasion."

"You're not hearing or seeing anything now are you?"

"No. I'm not. I'm not even ill right now. It does flare up sometimes, sort of like a bad back but with my mind. Times of stress are awful for me. Fortunately, I have a going creative business, so I am my own boss and I create when I can."

"That's wonderful," Silka said. "I'm happy for you and I know you must have spent many years to get to this point." She seemed quite comfortable glossing over my sins and getting to something more meaningful between us.

"My entire life just about. I have focused on my career and just in the past few years have I hit pay dirt. Creative careers are like that. I won't have to work again in this life if I choose not to. And I might not get the chance. The inspiration and the sweat involved can dry up overnight."

"So you have that much money. Oh, here's our waiter. Order for me. I'm going to the ladies' room."

"Will do." I watched Silka sashay off and thought that went quite well. *I think I've got a keeper,* I thought to myself. The realization was almost mystical and profound. *I may have found a new woman.* The moment stretched on for a long time, going by much more slowly than most moments. And then I remembered what I had to have. She had to believe in me. It seemed a nebulous concept and I did not know how it might play out, but a woman had to believe in me, or I was certain I would meet with a drastic and harsh fate. But that was it. That was all it took from her end was to believe in me and my bonds would be broken. She might, in effect, be my savior in a sense. And it appeared to be Silka. She appeared to be the one. I lost all train of thought and was wrapped up in the moment entirely, so much so I didn't realize at first that Silka had rejoined me at our table.

"What did you order for me?"

"A combination fish and scallops and veggie dish. Everything's fresh."

"Sounds delicious. I've been meaning to tell you something too, and now seems like the right time. I have a mentally retarded brother, and yes, I know they don't say it that way anymore, and he's in an institution in Jacksonville, and I kind of inherited his care. He got along with me the best anyway, but that was why I was crying on the stairs that day. Don't say you didn't notice."

"No, I noticed. Actually, I have heard you cry at night too."

"I guess the whole building has then. He's been arrested for beating up a woman that works at the facility. He's never been violent before and I don't know what has gone wrong. I'm thinking of pulling him out and having him with me. What do you think of that?"

"Well, first thing it is entirely your decision, and I'll support any action you take, but how old is he?"

"He's twenty-three. He was a late baby and mom tipped the bottle quite a bit back then. We weren't really sure. He doesn't talk much to my other brothers, so he stayed home with me and we get along. He's a nice kid really and he listens to me. You'll have to earn his trust. He's much smarter than you might think, but he can't really work at anything, but he does help around the house, or he did when we had a house. I don't know what he's going to be like in an apartment, or with a strange man around."

"We'll see how it goes, if you bring him here. What about the charges?"

"I think I can get the lady to drop them, if I pull him from the facility. So, we both had secrets. It's always like that you know."

"Yes, I suppose so. Here comes our food."

"Great," Silka said. She had worked up an appetite. We ate and talked off and on, and I could see her mind buzzing and rattling about with notions, but I paid a little less attention than perhaps I should have, but it was a pleasant lunch, so I did not feel quite as "en guard" as usual.

I wanted to stop by Reitz Gallery on my way home with Silka. I did not have with me my paintings that I would use to replace the others that were stolen, but I wanted to introduce Silka to Chanel. I would likely make out quite well now that there had been a robbery, depending on what Chanel had insured my paintings for. They were not her higher ticket items, but a few went for in the thousands, so I stood to make a good bit of money. I would not press for a check today, and Chanel would pay me when she got paid by her insurance company anyway. We had worked together quite some time and were loyal friends. Silka might benefit from meeting someone that I knew, and I had heard Chanel had hired a new assistant, a Russian gal named Tatianna. I wondered how versed this new assistant was in fine art, so if she was there I wanted an introduction. She was slightly younger than Silka, Chanel had told me, and as Chanel ran a class act, I assumed this new assistant knew what she was doing.

Chapter Seven

We arrived at Chanel Reitz Galleries, which was out of the way from home and my and Silka's apartments, and located in Winter Park, Florida, but then I needed to talk to Chanel and it was a nice day for a drive. It was the afternoon and the sun was nicely overhead and not sneering down at us. Silka did not have anything in particular to do after her interview and lunch, so I shanghaied her and took her to see what remained of my better pieces.

When I walked into the fashionable gallery surrounded by boutiques and fine antique stores on Corrine Avenue near Baldwin Park, I knew immediately there was almost nothing left hanging of my work. I hadn't quite believed the thieves were so interested in my accomplishments as Chanel had indicated over the phone.

"Christopher Devin," Chanel said "You look marvelous. And who is this?"

"My close friend Silka," I said. I introduced the two more formally and Chanel pulled Silka aside for dramatic flair and told her something about me.

"Hang on to this one, Silka. He's the devil to be sure, but a great man, and he does wonders, if you have not found out yourself as yet."

"I'm beginning to think so," Silka said. "After meeting his wife, it is nice to meet a friend of his."

"Clever girl, Chris, and she's beautiful. Dump Alison and hitch your star to this one," Chanel said.

"Already in the process, my dear. So I can see what they took or I guess I can see only what remains of what was taken. Or is that right? This is a befuddlement. I can't see what isn't there and it looks like a lot is no longer there." Mostly it was my works that were missing. I wondered why. "Why was I the target, Chanel?"

"Tatianna has a theory on that," Chanel said.

"Oh, may I meet her?" I asked.

"She's standing right behind you," Chanel said. Tatianna had slunk up close behind me.

"Tatianna, I am Chris Devin," I said spinning on my heels in proper military fashion with my right hand extended. "This is my friend Silka. A pleasure to meet you I'm sure," I said.

"Likewise. My theory has to do with the Madrid Art Show, Mr. Devin. You are not so well known in Europe as you are in Florida and the southeastern United States, and the show comes up in about two weeks. I think some of your works might be auctioned there."

"Hmm, possible I suppose. High intrigue. What would we do if that happens to be the case?"

"I've taken the liberty to alert some dealers I know in Europe. They will notify authorities if anything like that happens. And, of course, Chanel will be there as well."

Something did not sound right to me that Tatianna spoke. It put me on caution and I broke away from her and whisked Silka and Chanel down a hallway, saying a polite goodbye and that I did not wish to disturb her further as I was aware of work she might have to do. I thanked her too for her concern and the lengths she had gone to, ensuring that the thieves might be caught.

Telepathically, I spoke into Chanel's mind and asked if what Tatianna said was true. Again telepathically, Chanel answered she had heard Tatianna discuss the matter and it was an overseas call, and Chanel added she thought it was to Madrid, but she could not say for certain. I could distinguish Chanel's natural-speaking voice through our telepathy, a rare gift of mine that enabled me to know the source of the voice in my mind, and not have to attribute it to space clutter. I thanked her and expressed a bit of concern about her new assistant, which caught Chanel off guard a bit and she said she would keep an eye on Tatianna.

During all of this, Silka and I were taking in the view of some of the works of fine art, not all of which were by local artists. There were several exquisite pieces in the gallery, not to mention statuary and other *objets' de art* that were from clients in New York and Chicago. Chanel had cultivated a fine web of artists and turned her gallery in the process into one of the finer galleries in the state. Orlando is kind of a cow town, like most of Florida's cities, but Winter Park was a respite from that and there were people here with notable sensibilities about art.

Silka was favorably impressed and demonstrated as much. Not really one for the museums and galleries, she still had raw emotions to speak of and how the paintings in particular made her feel. If that is not the result of a good day in the studio and a tribute I would say as well to the artists, then I do not know what is. In the final essence, art is about how it affects the individual, most commonly how it affects the artist, but if there is a following, then why shirk the parades on Main Street. I enjoyed Silka's comments on some of the pieces. It was food for thought and it never hurts to look through someone else's spectacles on occasion.

A black Mercedes pulled into the small parking lot across from Chanel's gallery. It was quitting time. Tatianna polished up a last-minute request and told Chanel goodbye for the day. She got into the Mercedes, which belonged to my nemesis, Jude.

"You were right. He showed up today," Tatianna said.

"I knew he would. He's got something going on with Chanel. I don't know what it is, but you're going to find out for me. It's just another cast of the net. I'll pull the web in tight over this guy. I'm going to bring Chris to his knees. You watch. I'm going to ruin him. Like he did me."

"He's kind of nice. You can't just let it go? I mean he raped your wife and all, and she committed suicide, but how do you know that had anything to do with Chris's actions. It was years later she died and you were separated. If you don't want to talk about this, I understand."

"I don't. And I know. He's a sneaky, low-down cheating creep and I'm going to make him pay for what he did to my wife."

All this time that their conversation in the Mercedes continued, I could hear it in my head even though Silka and I were miles from the scene by then. We were both back at home, in fact. She had retired to her apartment to take a nap, and I had gotten on my computer and was looking at some stocks. I paid closer attention to what was being said in my mind, however. The man's voice that filtered through to my mind's ear had serious intent and I wondered what the true motives were. I could not tell who it was. I usually have to be in reasonable proximity to the person to hear his or her natural voice in my mind; otherwise, it could be from Adam or Eve and I wouldn't know usually who is saying what or why I should listen or care. This conversation drew my immediate attention. It was a bonafide threat.

I had heard them mention Chanel, so I knew it was someone that knew me or Chanel, and Tatianna seemed the likely suspect, but I was not sure if I detected an accent. I was able to tell it was a man and woman's voices. But the man said I had raped his wife, and, of course, I knew I had done no such thing ever in my life. Or at least in this current life of mine. I could not account for what I could not remember in a previous life. I wasn't worried for Chanel. She can take care of herself. Chanel had friends everywhere with their eyes and ears alert. It may seem strange, it does to me, but I am a little more defenseless on occasion than Chanel. So I was troubled by what I heard. And I wondered if I had unknowingly encountered a new enemy. The odds were stacking up against me.

I remembered something else I had to have from my savior. It was odd for me to consider that Silka, a slightly impulsive young woman in her early thirties might be my savior, but it may well be the truth. I had to hear her say the words, "I love you," to me. I had been set up by my father my entire life without so much as a true friend, except perhaps in grade school, or they were just inept enough at sabotaging me that we could get along in spite of matters. It all sounded so paranoid to me when I thought of it, but that was how it had been and pretty much up to the present day. Even my mother was driven insane at a formative time in my life, so I could not count on her guidance much. She did settle back down, however, and was not the irrational creature again she had been for years, but by then she preferred the door of the institution.

I went ahead and sold my natural gas stocks. It was closing in on February and the season was milder than usual up north, so it was time to unload them. At the same fell swoop I wrote a check to the Eugene Butler homeless shelter, my abode for nearly one year during a not-so-nice chapter in my life. The check was for five thousand dollars. I would pocket the rest from my stocks and put it in a certificate of deposit for the time being, as soon as the transaction closed. It would be nice to have some liquidity. Maybe Silka and I could go somewhere together.

Chapter Eight

I was summoned to Florida Hospital again. This time by the intensive care nurse. My father had lapsed into a coma and was on life support, and she and others wanted to know what I was going to do. I was not his healthcare surrogate, but I lied and said I was. The hospital staff never asked for proof. I would do his biding and pull the plug on him. I could not leave him on life support. It would run up a huge bill at the hospital that ultimately his estate, which he said he left to me, would have to pay for, and he could not move on to his next life as long as he was confined in a body in a vegetative state. I thought about leaving him that way for a long moment, but I couldn't. I was not ready for what happened nor will I ever forget it. It happened only the one time in my life.

I clasped his hand and told him I was at his bed. He blinked, which showed some awareness on his part, and I questioned my plan momentarily, but the intensive care nurse assured me that it was not unusual for that to happen, and he had no quality of life to return to, if he came out of his coma and go could off life support, both of which were big ifs. So I told her to pull the plug. He wanted me to do that for him, and the nurse said she would clean him up first. She meant removing the spittle from around his face and chin, and I could come back she told me in about fifteen minutes, and he would be off life support. She warned me it could take hours for him to actually die and I knew I needed to be there because of the doors he said that would open in my mind and I alone could guide him through the correct one he wanted to pass through.

So I went downstairs to the lobby of the hospital and got a cup of coffee. No doors had ever opened in my mind that I was aware of. I wondered if it was a trick. Was this all a hoax, I wondered? Was my father going to stuff me inside one of those doors and thus eliminate me? I worried he might try to usurp my life. I did not know what to think. I was still angry with him over the fact he had me hypnotized me into believing I was mentally ill, and as a result of the medication I took all those years I actually became mentally ill, or at least had certainly developed a dependence on the drugs. I might not have a mental illness at all and possibly never had one, but it sure felt as though I did. It had started in college, and as I have said he opposed my choice of college, saying it was my mother's choice for me to attend and not his. I had lived with my mother at that time. But the hypnotism was long before my college years, I assumed, since I did not have much to do with my father throughout that part of my life. My family life was always the biggest trick of all, and one that I had to navigate clearly or wind up abandoned or on the rocks. Each was a nagging reality that played over and over in my head from time to time. I could see the ship run aground and be battered against the rocks.

I tried not to think how much was in his estate and that I would inherit. I thought of my sister, Dinah. I had not heard from Dinah, but I knew she would be paying me a call. I went back upstairs after my coffee. The intensive care nurse said she was ready and he would pass quickly, which was merciful at least. I clasped his hand again and said, "I'll tell you when to pass dad…I'll do what you want this last time." He gripped my hand tightly it seemed for someone off life support in a coma and dying. Then I saw the doors. There were three of them down a long narrow hallway. I could see my father walk past the first door. Obviously, that was not the correct door. As he lay in the bed, his death bed, he grunted and gnashed his teeth and made an eerie whistling sound as he exhaled. The last two doors opened up simultaneously. From one came a pure white light that emanated into the hallway or corridor I guess I would call it. The other door exposed a jungle of ferns and rainforest and tropical trees so thick there was barely any room to enter.

I don't know why I did it. Maybe it was because these images were in my mind and seemed unreal somehow. I questioned the veracity of what I was seeing all the time, but knowing it mostly was true. I told my father to pass through the door with the jungle inside, understanding it was the wrong door for what my father's purposes were. And he did pass through it. I said, "that's it," as he approached the wrong door, and he drew his last breath as an old man, he went through the door, and was no more on earth. But he had to come back, and I knew he would. He and I had unfinished business that would be taken up in his next life, and possibly my next life as well. I had bought myself some breathing space. I hoped that much was true. I was not so invested in the consequences for my father, as I did not know what they were, but I was sure I would hear about them at some point.

My father had a habit of rabble rousing and kicking sleeping dogs, and I knew I was on borrowed time shortly after I left the hospital. He would be cremated and that would be an end of his body, and though I considered I might not see him again, I knew the worst between us was yet to come. I went down to my car, and there were police all over the parking lot. Father loved using certain police officers to intimidate people. I noticed my car was right in the middle of a taped-off area. The lettering on the tape read "Do Not Enter."

"That's my car in there," I said to one of the police officers on the scene.

"You'll have to wait," he said.

"How long?" I asked.

"About an hour maybe," he said. Then he changed his mind. "The suspect tried to enter your car. They will need you to open up your car, so they can look inside."

"Did he get in my car?"

"We don't know." The police officer then motioned to someone and said he's right here, indicating I was the owner of the car in question. I did not like this one bit. I respected the police and the job they did and thus tried to stay as far away from any of them as I could, but I went ahead and opened my driver side door and popped my trunk. The cop that looked in my car apparently didn't find anything incriminating, so he said I could go on my way. I thanked him and drove off under the tape as another officer held it up higher for me, knowing all the while my father had set this up beforehand. A whisper in the ear of some individuals was all it took for them to commit a crime, and temptation was a favorite tactic of my father's. I guess the man who was handcuffed in the back of a cruiser had wanted to get in my car and make a switch of vehicles, but the police were too fast for him.

Living in Florida as I do, there is something called the *Baker Act*, which mercifully allows police that are capable of such things to make a determination as to the mental well being of the suspect, or often the perpetrator of a crime. If he seems like he does not understand or the suspect has some crazy story, the police will take him to a city-run hospital with a psychiatric ward. I assume most states have similar legislation. I was Baker Acted four times one year before I was married, and that was what led up to my house being foreclosed and my year as a homeless person and then living in a homeless shelter for another year. I don't blame the police. I was going to be foreclosed upon one way or the other. The police merely sped up the process and took me to proper shelter rather than mix me in with the general population in jail. I had done no wrong. I was sitting on the Interstate one time, loitering around a gas station another, and out in the middle of a busy highway another time. Those types of behavior should land one in a mental hospital and they did me.

I really was looking for a way to die and if one is likely to do harm to himself or others, which is how that particular piece of legislation reads, then he gets the psych ward. And the doctors then deal with the problem, but it is a tough call for some police, but not as tough as one might think. The police have seen it all and they certainly know erratic or aberrant behavior when they see it. The time I was walking in morning rush-hour traffic, I got a feeling a friend had called the police on me. He or she had done me a favor, as had the police officer, a woman who knew how to handle me well. I am not rude to the police, and I have never fought one. They actually calm me down, if something has gone wrong. I find most of them know their jobs well.

As I was driving off, I realized I did not have much I had to accomplish this day. I wanted to see Silka and had thoughts of a picnic in the park. She too was just sitting by the phone, hoping for word about a second interview and I persuaded her to come with me and that we would get coffee first.

"So, here's a nice spot," I said. It was under an oak tree and the three fountains of friendship were busting out making their usual display. At night they lit the fountains with fiber optic lights and they changed into a multi-hued rainbow as the water cascaded down around the pond. The geese and pigeons were often aggressive but they kept their distance this time.

"My father passed away today. I was at the hospital earlier," I said.

"I'm so sorry. I had no idea. You never spoke of him before."

"We were not on the best of terms. He was an evil man. But not really a man. A god of sorts I guess you might call him. He and I did not see eye to eye on many things. I'm glad he's gone, but he'll reach me from the great beyond. Somehow I know he will."

"I'm here for you, but I have to say something and please don't take this the wrong way. You have been sounding so paranoid lately. I guess it is because of your illness. It disturbs me though."

"I'm sorry. I didn't realize. I have little control over that aspect of my personality. I'm conditioned to think in those terms, because of my mental illness, and because of who I am and the events of my life. My father was Satan," I said. I wondered how appropriate that remark of mine was at the time.

"All fathers have that bit of character to them. I loved my dad anyway. They are just people. They're human like anyone else."

I didn't want to go into further detail. "Let's enjoy our lunch."

I arrived back at my apartment and no sooner did the phone ring. It was my sister, Dinah. She must have learned that our dad passed and was trying to collect.

"Hey, so did he leave me anything?" Those were her first words. Nothing like how is it going? Or are you doing all right? Did he leave me anything?

"No, nothing. I don't know what is in the estate yet, but he had dared me to give you anything, so you know I can't."

"The asshole. Just float me a small loan. I'll pay it back. I've been clean for over a month now. I would have gotten in touch sooner, but I have a new boyfriend. And no, he's not a user."

"I wasn't going to ask." I knew what my sister was saying was a lie. "I'll think about it. It might be possible, but it will be my terms, Dinah or nothing."

"Okay. When do you meet his attorney?"

"Tomorrow," I said.

"Let me know. He was my father too. I should get something for suffering through with his miserable ass. I'm serious. Don't leave me twisting on this one."

"I won't. Bye." Dinah had not seen our father that I was aware of in over twenty years. I didn't know what she expected him to leave her, so I would find out if he really did leave her anything and was just bamboozling me. He was so shifty he might have left her everything. One thing was true. I met tomorrow with the attorney that my father had almost all his adult life. I was not looking forward to it, even though my father had indicated I was going to receive a good bit of money. I knew of his attorney. He was callous and mean.

It was a day of attorneys. It started with my divorce attorney, who phoned and said he had a court date and that my wife had been served with papers. He woke me up. I was an early riser usually, but had not been sleeping well, and I did not feel like creating or painting with all of what was going on in my life. The portrait of the man and woman still hung unfinished in my makeshift studio, the second bedroom of my apartment. I dragged myself out of bed and took a shower and decided to call Silka, and then thought better of it. I would see her later today. I dawdled over breakfast, a banana with peanut butter on it, and then set out to this hideous man's office.

His name was Hoinnekker. I think he was of German or Polish descent. He told me that my father was on the verge of bankruptcy due to his medical bills. I would have to take possession of the estate after parts of it went through probate, pay off the creditors to the tune of about one million dollars, and then I could keep what was left, minus the taxes. My father also had not paid income tax for the last four years, so there were lots of penalties. Hoinnekker said there was no way of telling if anything would be left but my father had named me as the sole representative of his estate, so I had to settle matters.

My father basically screwed me from his grave. *He must think this one is quite funny*, I mused. *I bet he has heard the entire conversation with his attorney and me*, I thought to myself. *Such a sense of drama he has*. I did not find it amusing at all, and supposedly there were some sort of court standards by which this estate had to be settled, or else I was in violation of the law, which did not rest well with me either. And Hoinnekker warned me that my father's wishes were that Dinah receive nothing; otherwise, there would be Hell to pay. And that was a direct quote from Hoinnekker, who probably encouraged my father and assisted him in setting up his estate this way. I wouldn't even get a fee for my services. I decided to go home and go back to bed.

I fell asleep without too much difficulty, but was rudely awakened by what sounded like someone in my living room. I called out to him and shouted that he better get out of here if he knew what was good for him. There was no reply and no further sounds emanating from any other room in my apartment, so I decided I had better check it out. It could have been a smash and grab. My exterior door was kind of flimsy. Snooker was squawking, but not loudly. I did not pick up my gun. I now always kept my loaded revolver on the nightstand. I went into my living room and found no one, so I checked the door to my apartment and it was unlocked. I could not remember if I had locked it or not. Dealing with attorneys had worn me out and I was still punchy. Nothing was missing. That was somewhat unusual for me—the unlocked door—as I am very conscious of my own security and would not normally forget to lock a door, especially if I was taking a nap or otherwise indisposed such as being in the shower.

Then I heard a noise coming from my bedroom. It was my twins. They were laughing this time as I re-entered my bedroom. At such an age—I really didn't know what age they were—if they needed attention from their father, they knew how to get it. They didn't ever speak to me, and they did not this time either, but rather made little noises so I would know it was them. They were an irritable pair occasionally, petulant girls, but more often festive and playful, but they needed encouragement from me once in a while. I referred to them as my F-44 Hornets. I would call out on occasion, "Where are my F-44 Hornets?" They would come blazing through the room faster than light and almost undetectable to me, except for the swish of air on either side of my ears, and one time I had made the mistake and I said, "let's play," and they attacked me very strategically and wore me out in under one minute.

A champion boxer would be hard pressed to stay in the ring with the likes of my girls. If they didn't hear from me what they wanted to hear, they would get ticked off and leave, and there would be no telling when they would come back or under what circumstances, so I said, "okay, play."

They laughed and shot little beams of light at each other from around the room. It looked like light sabers cutting through walls and furniture. It was quite magical. Here and there a flash would go off, similar to the flash of an antiquated flash on an old camera, and I guess that constituted a hit on one of their parts. They liked to think they were Jedi knights, or some facsimile thereof. But I could never trust if they were the true culprits or not. I was never sure it was my twins because they never spoke to me.

Sometimes they just showed up and confused matters. I could get very edgy when they showed up too. They were of me somehow, as in, I am their father and Alison is their mother, whom they will have nothing to do with as far as I know, but when they showed up, bad things could start happening in my life. It was good to have them nearby, however, because they did help me, even if they were very cantankerous at times. But then hornets have quite a sting. Snooker began raging more loudly. He could feel them and apparently did not approve of their antics.

I pondered whether someone had a key to my apartment other than me and possibly the maintenance man, who might have his own key, and just as I settled back down a bit, the phone rang and it startled me. I actually jumped it scared me so badly, and the hypnotic ring seemed much louder than I remembered it. It was Dinah.

"Hey, what's mine?" Dinah asked.

"Nothing, I am sorry to say. There's nothing left in his estate as near as the attorney could find."

"That's fucking bullshit. He had millions. I know it. I want my money. Don't screw me on this Chris or I'll kill you. I swear I will. He was my fucking father."

"I'll see what's left, but it is going to take some time to get the creditors and the IRS taken care of, and then I have to pay estate taxes on top of that, if there is anything left. This won't settle out overnight. Just wait and don't fucking threaten me with your bullshit threats. You can't do anything to me, Dinah, and you know it."

"We'll see about that," my sister said and slammed down the phone. Dinah turned to her lover. She was in bed with him and had placed the call from her bedroom in a shabby, but not altogether run down one-bedroom apartment. "You're going to have to kill him. I can inherit the estate if he's dead. We'll move somewhere better. Will you do it?" she asked her lover.

"Yeah. Let me handle it," he said.

Chapter Nine

"Chris, I want the house, but I can't afford it and they will only loan me one hundred and fifty thousand. I'll give you the one-fifty and take over the financing if you sign the house over to me in a quit claim deed. You can have your attorney draw it up," Alison said.

My wife had called and I had no idea how she had gotten my number. I closed my eyes and tried to see her, but failed. There were just lightening bolts crisscrossing with each other inside my closed lids and though I saw that frequently I never knew how to interpret it. It was something from beyond the earthly plane.

"The house is easily worth four hundred thousand and did you forget it was my money that paid it off? You're such a screw job, Alison. I hate your guts."

"Likewise. One-fifty…take it or leave it, and if you leave it, I contest the divorce. I know what you had those paintings insured for that were stolen from your little whore's gallery. I'll take half of that and make out like a bandit. I can only get one-fifty, Chris."

Who she had been talking to after the remark about Chanel and the insurance money, I had no idea. She might have been the one having me followed. She had nothing to do with my father. She thought it was all some grand story I concocted or a delusion that had gotten the better of me. He felt it was better to leave it that way, so he could endlessly upset her. He did too. She was always having one crisis after another. "I'll think about it, Alison, and get back to you." I hung up the phone. I knew I would agree just to get out of the marriage.

She turned to her lover and said, "I'm going to kill him. You can help me or I will find someone who can and you're out."

Alison's lover indicated he was in. She fell into his arms.

I decided to go to the park again only without Silka this time. It was a mossy, tree-strewn drive with old oaks jostling for position twenty feet over the road. The Dragon's breath was in bloom, pink and yellow, and garbage cans lined the sides of my little drive out to the boulevard. The blue recycling bins accentuated the grayish cans on the green grass and dotted the highway here and there.

And then two black SUVs pulled up next to me at a traffic light. One was behind me and the other to my side, effectively boxing me in. They would have just assassinated me if they wanted. One man with an automatic weapon would jump out and spray lead my way till I slumped forward. It was always like that in the movies. It was like that in real life too. There was no point in running. They could be anywhere I was going in advance of my even knowing I was going to a particular destination. My father could peek around the corner of time, which made it so difficult to escape his grasp. I stood my ground and tried not to panic. I looked over, and I saw the driver to my right make a cell phone call.

"He's on Pearl Street. Yeah, I'm right next to him at the light. He's going to Friendship Park, I think. No, I am certain."

I could hear every word the man next to me at the traffic light said. These were not my father's men. They were of a different ilk. Someone really was keeping tabs on me and it was by way of their cell phones. It seemed kind of primitive. My father's men did not need cell phones. They were as highly telepathic as I am and probably had more of a range. And I could never usually get inside their minds unless they spoke to me first. Of course, this man was speaking out loud, but his driver-side window and my passenger-side window were raised. This was not a fortunate circumstance. So Jude or Alison were up to nasty tricks, and they were slow to show their hands this time because probably they wished to create an air of terror in me. But I was not really that afraid once I realized they were not sent by my father. He certainly by now knew he had been duped on his death bed. I might have sent him somewhere he was likely to get lost for quite some time. I hoped, in fact, he would never come back, but I didn't think I would be that lucky.

I left the spot after the light turned green and changed my direction further down the boulevard. I was going into the heart of the city's slums over off Highway 40. I might get a beer and then head back home. Let's see if these valiant men in their shiny SUVs were brave enough to follow. As I suspected, they turned off. Nothing like a slum to find out who your friends are. I felt bad for the poor. They were the ones most deserving of something from the government and always the last ones to get it.

I pulled up into the parking lot of a rough leatherneck-looking sports bar. I was sure it held black male denizens mostly, but I did not care. Black men in particular never trifled with me. I left them alone and didn't make any messes that involved them, and they left me alone. Father hated black men and he did everything he could to them. And he adored black women, so it was easy to have a certain few female African Americans do any and everything to their partners, and father could relax and laugh about it later.

It had to do more with a perceived spiritual nature of African American men, rather than any religious issues. Father loved religions, all of them, because he swore they were all false and he swore to me that he had invented them all. He was in church every Sunday and he could quote every line of the Bible. He loved to sing along with the hymns and the choir, and at one particular church everyone thought he was an assistant pastor. He could bi-locate as frequently as he needed. That in and of itself is a miracle and he could make miracles happen. Who said all miracles were of God or even that great a thing. I think most miracles are often terrible things.

He would have loved nothing better than to see the return of the Holy Church ala the Middle Ages. The Middle Ages was a grand time for him, he told me once, with so much controversy and so few literate people and so many desperate and poor. And he cared nothing about Christianity. He saw it as a burden for the believers, who no matter what they did always came up short, which he found most amusing. Father loved the concept of original sin. That and crack cocaine were favorite inventions of his. He never claimed any authorship of the Bible that I know of, but it wouldn't surprise me if he had written a chapter or two. He had his hands into everything and weaved a tangled web.

So I got a beer and then another and tipped the barkeep well, and said a polite goodbye and headed out the door. No events took place, no one spoke to me, nothing unusual happened, and that made my mind a little calmer. There were no shiny SUVs in the parking lot. I might have eluded my prospective captors and I might also have figured out or narrowed down who they were, but I did not yet know why someone was screwing with me. One thing was certain: they would either get theirs or I would get mine, however that might play out. I no longer cared as much which side won, me or the other hell-bound bastards because the pressure in my mind was starting to get to me and acting in a normal, reasonable, rational fashion was becoming more difficult though there were no overt signs that I was losing my grip. Not yet.

While I was celebrating my small victory, as to eliminating my father's handiwork from contention, there was another conspiracy brewing across town I was unaware of. I heard nothing of the conversation and never knew it existed until much later.

"Get her to go to lunch with you. She might be useful. Pump her for info, anything useful…what he does as his routine, where he goes, when he is home working, things like that, okay?"

"Yeah, I'll do it, but I don't like this," Tatianna said. "You're using me as some sort of spy, and I am not a spy. Besides she's a pleasant girl. She has very little to do with what's between the two of you, Jude. They just met."

"I know, but I have a longstanding score to settle and then you're done. Do this one thing, and I won't ask for anything else. I may not kill him, but I am sure going to lower his standards."

"You're making me an accomplice to this. What are you going to do to them or to him? I want to know."

"Just rattle his cage and try to get him to run out of town. He was born here and he doesn't want to leave. He knows this entire city just about. If I could disgrace him enough somehow that he would have to leave then that would be plenty. That's my job. I can't go around calling him a rapist. I don't have any proof. It's slanderous sounding and he might take me to court on that one, and I don't want that," Jude said. Jude was thinking to himself of exactly what he was going to do. He was going to have Chris killed. But he was not going to tell Tatianna the truth.

Even though they slept together and she practically lived with Jude, it was none of her business as he saw it. She could finagle her way out of legal complications if this went down the wrong way, so why not use her to help accomplish his goal. He was getting tired of Tatianna anyway. The sex was good, but she was too pushy. Jude did not open up much; he never had really, and the alcohol he hid around his house, so he could conceal how much he actually drank, had made him more secretive and stealthy. He was starting to find life with Tatianna depressing, or so he thought it was because of her.

Tatianna was younger, and he had hoped more malleable in personality, and a very good-looking lady, but his heart was turning cold toward her. She, of course, was also growing dissatisfied as his girlfriend. Jude had seemed so loving and tender in the beginning, but that part of their relationship had rubbed away quickly. She was beginning to resent the fact that he was involving her in his vendettas. She found Chris an agreeable man and handsome and polite. In fact, she liked him, and the little smattering of conversation she had had with Silka had gone well too.

Tatianna began to feel a deep-seated anger that she could not express to Jude. Resentment will kill the good feelings in a relationship quicker than anything, and Tatianna knew this. And that was what she felt about having to go through the motions of supporting Jude against a local artist that the two of them, Chris and Jude, had some minor disagreement in high school over twenty years ago. It was ridiculous, and then and there she decided she would not do exactly what Jude wanted. She had her own plan. And she was angry. Angry with Jude.

As soon as Tatianna had extricated herself from Jude, she made a phone call to Silka and invited her to lunch that same day, and Silka accepted the invitation. It was more of a coffee house that served chic, artsy-type sandwiches. These places were often referred to as boutique restaurants by the locals because they were elaborately appointed and catered to upscale clientele. The place had a courtyard with a fountain and tropical greenery, and was surrounded by clothiers and an exotic candy shop and apartments up above. The metal table and chairs by the fountain were inviting spots to sit, and the small rush of a cool, slight waft of air swam through the breeze blowing off the street. The coffee house was nearby Chanel's gallery and Tatianna was on her lunch hour. She watched as Silka walked in the main room first, and then greeted her as she came outside to the courtyard. They ordered their meals and chatted about Tatianna's work for a few brief moments. Silka did not know this woman, and guessed the appointment for lunch was set up by Chanel or Chris as something to distract her mind and give her something to do.

Then Tatianna made a bit of a pained expression. "There's something I meant to tell you, dear," Tatianna said. "It's not good news."

"Oh, what's that?" Silka asked.

"My boyfriend hates your boyfriend because of something that happened a long time ago, and I know this sounds silly, but I think he's meaning to harm him."

"Silka laughed. "Everyone is so creeped out by Chris. He's a neat guy. I really like him. He's a little strange, but he's brilliant. And an artist. Artists are always that way. Artists and scientists. You should know that. At least that is what Chris tells me. I've never really known an artist before. You know he told me the other day his father was Satan. I had no idea things between them were so bad. I loved my father. Chris' father just passed on, and he has never said a word to me about his mother, other than she is in an institution. He doesn't visit often, I'm pretty sure," Silka said. "Anyway, any old business between your boyfriend and my boyfriend is in the past. Let's keep it there, and between us, let's just see if we can be friends. I appreciate the offer of lunch. I'm kind of new here. Chris shows me around some, and I am waiting to see if I have a job I applied for, but everything else is up in the air with my life. Chris is a big boy. He can handle himself. We'll just never put the two together, which suits me fine. I can use a close girlfriend," Silka continued.

"But I am serious. He really wants to harm him."

"Well, Chris will have to deal with it. I can't do anything about it. I'm not going to even mention it to Chris. He's been acting a little stranger than normal lately. He's moodier. Why does he want to harm my boyfriend?"

"He claims Chris raped his wife a long time ago, but I am beginning to wonder if that's true," Tatianna said.

"I'm sure it's not. Chris is a gentle man. I would have picked up on something like that. Is your boyfriend mentally ill too? You know, Chris has a mental illness and a wild imagination, and why not? It suits him. He probably could not paint without one. He's pretty paranoid though. It gets hard to take."

"No, he's an alcoholic. He hides rum bottles in the toilet. I always know there's one there, so I don't even look anymore. He doesn't know I know."

"That's bad. My mom in her later years drank a lot. I have a challenged brother because of her drinking I guess during her pregnancy. And I've got to make a decision soon as to what I am going to do with him. I am hoping I get this job so I can stop living off my inheritance, which has dwindled a bit, because if I do, I'll bring my brother here to live with me. No one else in the family wants him. He's a sweet kid, but he can be demanding."

"How's this sound?" I said. "All-expenses-paid weekend in Daytona Beach, the world's most famous and infamous beach. At least it used to be, but it's still nice. I got us a hotel room on the ocean, we can walk the beach, and it's only about an hour's drive. The hotel has a tiki bar ocean side too. What do you say?"

"Pretty good, I guess. Let's do it. Do you need to get away because I'm still waiting to hear about my interview?" Silka said. "But I guess I could call them. They're not likely to call on the weekend, are they?"

"No, probably not, but dropping your name in the hat again and asking if they have had time to make a decision wouldn't hurt."

"Okay, I'll try to find out today. What are you going to do?" my close friend and lover asked.

"I don't know. I don't have a plan for today. It's early. I might go up to my studio and try to paint."

"That would be good. Please try anyway."

"I am. No calls until after noon, okay?"

"Sure, see ya. Give me a kiss," Silka said and I then got out of her bed, walked downstairs and went into my apartment. I could not paint, however. I did not even try. I did not even walk into my studio. There was no point in trying; I would only destroy what I was working on. One mistake could be hidden in a painting, but not multiple ones, and I had not felt the gift lately. Pushing things with artistic expression was always a bad idea. Instead, I turned on the television in my apartment and watched the stock market. The overnight markets, that is to say the Asian markets, had closed down, so it was a good probability that the US stock market would have a down day. I lost interest shortly after the markets opened and just sat there.

I wasn't afraid exactly. I knew my end was near. I did not want to be the next Lucifer. I did not have it in me. Only Silka could save me from that fate now, and she thought everything I told her was hogwash and there was no way I could convince her. I wasn't even sure if I should try, or if she simply had to come to believe on her own that I was a good guy and not some sort of monster like half my city believed. And naturally I was trapped here. I could not get away for long, though I left Orlando frequently. I also always returned. And I had ended the habit of trying to move away every so often. It never got me anywhere when I was in my twenties, except broke and looking for a cheap place to stay. That's no way to go through life.

Chapter Ten

She was all of five feet tall, black hair so dark it was actually streaked blue and a look of steel in her eyes to match her downturned lips when she laughed. The lids to both eyes drooped a bit and gave her a weary, careworn look and partially hid from view her coal-colored irises. Her name was Kim, short for Kimberly; she was in her thirties, and an Asian temptress with an accomplice. She was really a phantom and not who Chris thought she was. Her accomplice was a jovial man who had no hatchets to bury in this world. He, too, was a phantom.

He was a red-bearded, red-headed Scottish gent who laughed easily and often. If it happened to be unknown what he did for a living, and so few did know his real vocation, most would consider him an intelligent, likeable man. He answered to the name Roddy. They were here to kill Chris. The pair were hired guns straight off a cleverly disguised Internet website, and they had been paid in full, it would appear, and came with glowing recommendations. Chris knew nothing of this when the deal went down.

Jude knew a lot of sordid types he could call upon, but he was smart enough to use them just for suggestions otherwise they would know his plan. He was not going to involve a local hit man for this job. Jude was still vulnerable and frightened of what might happen to him. He had kept his secret a long time. Jude was the older half-brother of Chris and he hated Chris far more than either of them was aware. Jude's father, the Prince of Darkness—Chris' father, the Prince of Darkness, had fooled both families. Satan alone had told Jude who Jude was and had told him that Chris had usurped his birth right, and Jude was the one in line to be the next Prince. To accomplish this Jude had to kill Chris. It was all a lie, but Jude believed it. Satan had no other son than Chris.

Kim had flown in from Los Angeles and Roddy had flown in from New York. They were a team, and no one knew how many kills they had between them, but the pair, if they bothered to remember such insignificant details. Jude had mailed a check in full payment to the host of the website, and though he had never done anything like this before, he felt he needed vengeance that badly, but could not convince himself to pull the trigger. He was scared to fire upon his own flesh and blood. Jude's entire life had been a lie, just as Chris felt his had been.

The team's *modus operandi* was to fly in and lay low, survey the surroundings and get acquainted with the mark's schedule. They rushed nothing and always guaranteed their work. She had that look in her eye that said, *watch out*, and he was an affable older man with grandchildren. Such an unlikely pair of assassins is in part what ensured their success. They would stay at separate hotels, meet only behind closed doors, and they never used cell phones. They always flew coach, and they packed carry-on luggage only. It might take a week or thirty days, but they felt confident they could always get the right person even in a sea of tourists like Orlando. That actually made this job easier. Tourists were simple to eliminate, and they knew their man was a hometown boy. They would look up his vehicle registration, get his address, then find his telephone number without saying a word about it to anyone but each other and scarcely that much would be said. They needed only to lay low and wait.

"What do you want for dinner?" Chris asked.

"How about frozen pizza?" Silka said.

"We'll have to go to the store. If you'll go in, I'll pay for it."

"Deal. You're going to have to stop avoiding people, Chris. They are a fact of life. I know you feel miserable when you can't paint. It's just a dry spell. All artists have them. You said so yourself."

"I know, but for right now, you go in and I'll stay in the car."

"I said I would. What are you afraid of?" Silka asked.

"Everything at the moment. I'm being followed, Silka and I don't know by whom."

"It's nothing. It's your chemicals. Redirect them in your brain and make it so you can paint again. You never finished that piece with you and me in it. It's all bad chemicals. Do you need to go to the hospital?"

"No. They would find me there," Chris said. "C'mon. I'll drive." We motored the quarter mile to the grocery store and Silka went in and I sat and wondered and thought.

She just doesn't understand. No one I know except Chanel gets any of this. And before I was married, Chanel and I tried to make it together. It just didn't work. We were too much alike. I wish it had, but there must have been plenty of reasons for my solitude. I got a lot of work done at any rate. Chanel was great. She just did not need me. Silka needs me more than Chanel did. Silka has this terrible fear of being abandoned. But she's not stupid. I can tell she will bail out if she has to. And why shouldn't she? And Silka has got to be the one. She must be, which means I might die soon. That was what father told me. The only way he would spring me from Hell's duty, is if a woman loved me. I guess he knew what to tell me, so I would believe him. Everyone has used me up to this point, but not Silka. She is actually interested in me and my work.

Something rudely stirred me away from my thoughts and recriminations. My international translator must have been on because I could hear two men approaching the grocery store who had to be speaking in some foreign tongue. They were dressed in grimy, greasy workman's jeans and t-shirts, carelessly and offensively so. I would guess the language was Greek, but I could not be sure. I mention my translator because I heard a perfect translation in English. I don't speak or understand much Greek at all. The two men planned on robbing the store, and one of them had a gun. They were discussing last-minute details of the heist that was about to take place. I knew I had to act, and act swiftly to get Silka out of there. They were standing by the front entrance, outside, and I could see the bulge in the one man's waistline. They were real criminals, rough looking and kind of crazy in the eye like some men get, and desperate, like the hunted. I had to find Silka. I assumed she would be next to the frozen foods and she was. I walked up to her and whispered in her ear, "Just listen…don't speak. The store is about to be robbed. Let's get out of here now."

"Are you for real?"

"Yes, damnit. Let's go."

"Okay, okay. I'm going." Silka looked right at the two men as we exited. They paid no attention to her. They had nothing to do with my father. They were ordinary rabble, and they were about to effect their legacies by leaving and getting caught in a high-speed chase and then both of them shot to death because they fired upon the police. It would take only minutes for the entire story to play out and I knew the ending and that

I had gotten Silka out alive and unharmed. She thought I was joking. She thought I was showing signs of greater paranoia until I insisted we watch the eleven o'clock news together that evening.

"It's them. I knew they would be on."

"How did you know that?" Silka asked. It's the two guys outside the grocery," she said. Then she started paying attention. "My God, they robbed the place. You were right. You heard them outside the store. How?"

"I have good ears," I said.

"You might have saved my life," Silka said.

"You will repay the favor, dearest, when the time is right. You have to believe me. I am a good man, damnit. In spite of what all the white trash in this fucking city think."

"Okay, okay, I'll try, but things are getting nutty around you and me. I have started feeling like I'm being followed too. An Asian woman in a Honda keeps popping up wherever I am going. And then she does nothing but sit in her car. She is always off at a distance, but I see her often enough. And Tatianna said her boyfriend wants to harm you. I wasn't going to tell you, but now I think I should."

"Who's her boyfriend?" I asked.

"I don't know. She said he claims you raped his wife."

"Ah, I know who's behind that myth. Beware of Tatianna. She might be a wolf in sheepskin."

"I don't think so. She was trying to help us. I think she was being honest and wants to avoid a problem if there's going to be one. I am no drama queen, Chris. High intrigue is not how I function. Have you forgotten I am from farm country? I am a farmer at heart. I may seem sophisticated, but it's because I rarely had a boyfriend and have read every classic novel and everything else there is."

"I know, my dearest. And I did not drag you into this. Others did, not me. You might be right about Tatianna though. We are definitely getting away for the weekend. Sleep here in my apartment tonight. The bed is comfortable."

"Okay, I'll get a few things and be right back."

"And Silka, dear, you can always count on Chanel to protect you if something bad happens to me. She will always help you."

"Okay, I'll be right back."

I put my revolver inside my night stand. I didn't want to frighten Silka needlessly at this point. She said things were getting nutty. They were likely to get a whole lot nuttier before it all ended. Silka returned and we bedded down for the evening. First I checked the outside door of my apartment and made sure it was locked. I stuffed a perfectly cut and sized two-by-four under the doorknob. My last thought that night was that my court date for my divorce was approaching. What a mess everything had become and all at the same time. Silka was my only bright spot.

We made the trek to the beach. Promoters of Daytona Beach had for the longest time extolled the virtues of Daytona Beach and were well known for saying it is the world's most famous beach. A great number of movies had been shot on Daytona Beach. Now, it is kind of run down and seedy, a little too rough of a place to get out much and mingle, but still a good vacation spot. The locals are not that friendly anymore, not like they were in the decades of the sixties and seventies. They resent the intrusions of Spring Break and bikers' week more and more, though many residents' livelihoods are based on those few short weeks.

Silka was surprised I owned a revolver. I pulled it out and showed it to her before we went to sleep that first night in the hotel. That didn't go very well. I assumed she would be relieved that I packed some kind of protection, and I had never even considered that most people are unwilling to trust a mentally ill man with a handgun. Alison had never said a word about it. I think she wanted to use it on me one time, but I woke up. I sleep with my eyes open. I'm not sure why that stopped her. The first time Silka saw me asleep with my eyes open she thought I was dead. It terrified her. She shook me trying to wake me up and I came out of my sleep and jumped up and said, "What?" Silka screamed even louder, and I was scared to death that someone had done something to her. We had a good laugh afterwards, but it was harrowing moment. As new as our relationship is to each other, I have already put Silka through a few twists and changes.

I don't mean to do this. It comes with the territory if someone gets close to me. That is why no one has ever stuck around, except Alison. We wound up hating each other. And she only did because she anticipated I would inherit a large sum of money. She had met my father and seen his lavish lifestyle, and did not even realize who he was. Alison liked him, in fact, but he hated her. He thought she was a common bimbo and he said as much to me. He referred to my wife as "that whore."

Alison also hoped I would use the gun on myself. I had attempted suicide before, twice actually, but the two attempts were a long time ago. They were honest efforts, but in the back of my mind I knew I would fail. I was in a coma the second time, and woke up and was released from the hospital the next day. It is never the right time to go until it is the right time to go.

The stay at the beach was nice. It took my mind off things. I didn't notice any of the men with cell phones clamoring around me, and Silka said afterwards that she did not see the Asian woman, so that made me think it was all local traffic and confined to Orlando. They, whoever it was that were after me, might not even have been aware we got away. The SUVs I noticed seemed normal and not as much of a threat.

So we came back from Daytona Beach and Silka did a strange thing. She started to avoid me. She was tied up when I wanted for the two of us to get coffee. Lunch became inconvenient for her. She blamed it on her job. She had gotten a job at a fancy boutique, not the original women's dress company at the mall. It was a much better job that she had gotten. The commissions were higher and the clothes cost a lot more, and the store catered to a very smart-looking, upscale clientele. Silka looked wonderful in the fashions of the boutique. She could not afford to buy them, but the owner had sent her home with a few of the fashions so she could see and feel how they were. It was a clever enough idea, but such a temptation to any woman to dig into her purse was a bit unwarranted. Silka looked stunning in the clothes. She could take something straight from the rack and try it on and it would always fit her perfectly. Silka said that Tatianna had put her onto the job, and had told her manager about Silka.

I let Chanel know this one day, as we were conversing on the telephone. We could communicate telepathically as we spoke on the phone. It was something similar to having two conversations going on simultaneously at the same dinner table. The conversations would bleed over and spill into each other and one would say something in a parallel conversation that would be an answer for something in the conversation of the others present. Even though I had not been a couple much of my life, I had noticed how this happened often. Only I did this with my mind, and Chanel and I had done this for quite some time. Chanel and I were not confined by a range either. We could do this all over the world with each other at different ends. It was something we chose not to do very much. It becomes a matter of privacy and a need to shut down one's mind.

I told Chanel that Tatianna seemed okay, and that maybe I had misjudged her originally, all the time jabbering about Daytona and Silka. Chanel just mentioned by way of our minds that Tatianna was doing a good job. And she left it there. I knew not to intrude further.

Finally, after being put off by Silka for almost a week and having limited phone conversations, I decided I would drop in at her apartment. We had not been spending every night together, but it had been most nights, even though Silka was a very independent young woman. She would simply say that she needed sleep and slept better alone. That was enough to get off the hook from spending every night with me, and I knew not to push on the subject. But she had never gone this long without sharing my bed in one way or another since we had met.

I knocked on her door and a young man opened. He spoke with deliberate, but difficult garbled pronunciation. I could tell immediately he was her brother.

"I'm Chris. You must be Hinton," I said.

"Yes," he said. He stood there waiting for his sister. Silka came into the room.

"Hi," she said.

"Is he why you have not called me?" I was actually relieved because I thought I was losing Silka, and it occurred to me that I might not be.

"He can understand things like that," Silka cautioned me.

"I'm sorry. I thought you were angry with me because I dragged you into my messy affairs."

"No, I'm not angry, but it has me worried for you and a little for me, and now for Hinton. Always use his name if you speak about him. Hinton understands better and he doesn't become as frustrated," Silka said.

"Okay, I will. How are you settling in Hinton? Do you like it here?"

"Yes," he said.

"Hinton was in Des Moines with one of his brothers recently. Wasn't that cool?"

"Yes," Hinton said.

"Let's do something after I get home from work tonight. What do you say, Chris?"

"Definitely. The three of us. Would you like that Hinton? How about the zoo?"

"Yes," Hinton said and he smiled a bit. His teeth were yellow and he did not blink often, and he had a large head for his body, even though he was obese, but he looked like a sweet young man, and I took a bit of a liking to him.

"Okay, tonight then. Give me a kiss, darling. I have to go figure out what I am going to do with my days now that you are working. I can drive out to the zoo and get us tickets. There's that much. Can Hinton stay inside on his own?"

"Oh, yes, Hinton can fix a sandwich and watch television or play music. Hinton's a little hard of hearing so he might play it kind of loud, so ask him to turn it down. He will. I don't want the other neighbors to be offended," Silka said. "The lady at the facility where he was staying was glad to get rid of him. Luckily, my brother took him for a little while."

We went to the zoo that evening and Hinton gazed at the baboons with such wide wonder. He smiled and was animated and he didn't want to leave to see any of the other animals. So we watched the baboons for an hour. It was about all I could take though a pleasant diversion. The baboons were quite animated themselves. A few strange people made queer remarks about me. It was not the cell phone users per se. These remarks were denizens of my city that I did not know of, but they apparently knew of me. And they seemed to not like me much. I passed over their comments which were always something petty and judgmental.

The cell phone followers were there at the zoo as well. I could not go anywhere in the city without someone communicating to Jude as to my whereabouts and what I was doing. It started out more discreetly, but as I ignored the intrusion more and more, those that reported on my leisure activities became easier to discern, more understandable and more within earshot. Silka had not as yet pieced these two separate parts of the puzzle together and I didn't want her to, simply because she would become frightened, and I did not want her scared. I expected my day was upon me sooner than it actually was to come, but all evidence pointed in the direction that my assumption was correct—I would die soon.

We got ice cream after the zoo, and Hinton and I became more like buddies: pals I would say. We bonded the old fashioned way at the dinner table, or parfait table as it was, and he did seem a lovely young man with something just short of an adolescent's mind.

And then something else struck me as funny. It was a voice from a long way off. The voice was familiar, and it spoke in French. I hallucinate in several languages, but they are not all hallucinations. Only some are, and determining which was which was tricky and I needed to be shrewd. I did not identify until later whose voice it was, but I was certain that the population of creamery and confectionary-goers had nary a word of French among them. No one nearby was speaking into my mind. The local mental midgets could not speak French, even if they studied it every day after cutting the lawn.

I had nothing truly against the hard-working, laboring men of the city; I just did not get along with the rabble. And there were plenty of hard-working lads to go around, but only some I would consider as belonging to the masses. The men and women who cut yards and were factotums, or otherwise worked crappy jobs with the theme parks, in my opinion, were not really a concern of mine. I was literate, an artist and not a Christian for obvious reasons, so I had nothing to say to these fair ladies and gentlemen. I found the trashy ones repulsive. I no longer even glanced in their direction. I remember a man stuffing cokes into a machine took issue with me one time for what reason I do not know. It was in a doctor's office and as he dribbled the last piece of change into a bucket I ordered him to take his pay and get out. It seemed very amusing to me. What a silly job for a grown man to do. If he had been fourteen, I might have understood. I recall how proud he was that he carried three cases of soft drinks at one time. He asked me if I was capable of doing that. I laughed. He was a numbskull.

I had started out where they were. I had been a laborer for many years, cutting grass, swinging from scaffolding, that sort of thing. Some chose to stay at those jobs and remain in that station of life and that was none of my business and certainly up to them, but it was not for me. They criticized me often for being mentally ill though it certainly was not my preference or fault. They shot disapproving glances, moaned demonstrably when I came in their workplaces, but I was undeterred. If I wanted a cup of coffee, I was certainly having one, and if a member of a certain establishment bemoaned the fact that I patronized the place and contributed to their wages, I would, of course, show up every day until I felt a sufficient point had been made.

I knew what was said in French, though it has been some time ago, I spoke the language. "*Prenez garde les ides de Mars.*" I could determine this was beaming in from another part of the world. I was transfixed momentarily and could not make out what Silka was saying, but luckily she was addressing Hinton. I sat there and closed my mind in a way and enjoyed my ice cream. The voice had said to *beware the ides of March.* Those were words spoken to Caesar before he was killed by Brutus and others. It was mid-February and March was closing in.

I was distracted again. Too much seemed to be flooding my senses and I was afraid of going on overload status, and losing my grip in a public place. But there was something else that had changed. It was a good thing. There was a certain light in Silka's eyes that had not been there before. I did not misinterpret it. She was happy having her brother with her and she was pleased the two of us, or now, the three of us, were getting along so well. She spoke with a little less tension in her voice and her mind was less cluttered. She was easing up more in demeanor and starting to have some fun even amidst the hot water in which I was increasingly finding myself. I did not blame her for that. I cherished it because she looked upon me as well with the new light in her eyes. It is a very special thing to see a woman so radiant. It occurs, but not so often, and only years ago had it occurred in my life, and there plainly was a gaze of fulfillment that Silka now had, and seemingly a sense of family that had lacked possibly from her life for some time. I could tell how much she loved her brother as she doted on him a bit. They were close, and it must have broken her heart to leave him behind in an institution, not knowing if he would ever live with her again.

I realized I had to do something, something extraordinary, and I was not sure I could pull it off. I was going to put Silka in my eyes. She would effectively be able to see what I saw, but possibly not even know it was from a different source than what she would normally see. If it did not work properly it could cause some confusion. Doing something such as this needed to run below a certain threshold of awareness, and if I was successful, Silka might not even know I had done anything at all, but I could more fully protect her this way. It was clearly a defensive measure designed to keep Silka from harm. That was the sole purpose. I thought about it, meditated just a bit and then saw something from Silka's direction come across to me on the other side of the table, where we sat in the confectioners. I guessed I had done it. I didn't feel any different and I saw what I usually saw with my eyes. None of my images had changed. I would check the bathroom mirror at home when I got back because I could see if I had succeeded. I would see her always in my eyes until I took her out. I had never done this before. I was beginning to fall in love.

Chapter Eleven

I had an interesting dream. It involved a company that was going to affect a minor miracle in medicine. And though I doubt I was on earth when I was involved with investigating the matter in my dream, I decided upon waking that there must be some company here that was doing exactly what I had seen. The device was a hospital bed, but it was no ordinary hospital bed. The hospital bed I saw could go from room to room and even straight into surgery on a moment's notice. It hovered and had a noiseless motor with a fan, something like on an air boat, and changed direction at the flick of a finger and a nurse or attendant could push it down the hall with complete ease. Furthermore, the doctors loved it, so I knew it was a hot ticket or would be, if still in design or soon to be in design. I just had to find out who was manufacturing it locally, so to speak.

There's a few funny lines from a movie comparing the US and Europe saying that there are essentially the same things on both continents, "It's just the little differences that matter, like a quarter-pounder with cheese is called Le Gran Royal." That is not an exact quote, but close enough, and all I could remember at that time of morning. It is like that through parts of the universe, where I go, but often do not have any recall afterwards of where I have been or how to get back there. I am sure there is good reason for that. There are the same things in other places, such as physical structures, environments, a controlling star, even something more mundane like a shopping mall or automobiles. Or to break matters down more, say just walls of glass and concrete or wood of some variety. They may be heavily barricaded or just a regular wall as found in a house or public building.

Only where I had seen the hospital bed, I noticed the walls were self-painting. Lines of green, blue, red and yellow dashed and danced around the floor and up the partitions, giving each a distinct color pattern and changing that color pattern with such ease it defied any human being's ability to paint that quickly. The lines seemed to be racing with one another, and it was not dizzying, but rather something marvelous to behold. And these were not masterpieces of art, merely painted walls, but so sublimely accomplished it gave pause. "It's the little differences that matter."

I awoke early and got up out of my bed and wrote down the hospital bed idea because the technology was already here, and wouldn't that be a grand invention of someone's, or was so already. I had to find the company working on the prototype and sit back for a few years till it went public or perhaps was bought out, and I might even get in on the initial price if the company came to market, assuming it was not already a public company with traded stock.

I thought of something else as well. Silka. I wanted to buy her roses today. I had not gotten anything like that, not even candy, and of course "Candy is dandy, but liquor is quicker." Words I lived by before when I was a single man. I, however, had in mind a baker's dozen of American Beauties. There was a floral shop not far down the road from my new apartment. I was beginning to learn this side of town. I liked florists. I had no bad associations with florists. I could care less if any of them were gay; I liked going to floral shops, and always when I did it meant I had a woman I at least trusted. I had bought Chanel and my soon-to-be ex-wife flowers all the time. If a florist was involved it was a happy time for me. Slaving at painting and getting nothing done and having no fun, and worse having no money with which to have some fun was a terrible predicament for me, as it decreased my creative abilities. It upset me chemically and I could not produce, but this was not a time like that. I had a fabulous new woman and I intended to spoil her rotten.

I walked up to Silka's apartment, my flowers discreetly held behind my back. Silka was crying. She seemed so emotional lately. Touchy was the word. I immediately wondered if I had offended her somehow, but I hadn't seen her in a couple of days, so I dismissed that notion as social paranoia.

"What's wrong?" I asked.

"Oh, it's my brother, the youngest one. He has flown through his part of the inheritance and he's asking me for money. He has a bad drinking problem. He wants to borrow five grand he says to buy his own taxi. He moved to Kansas City. I don't believe him, and it pisses me off that he is lying. He's a bad risk."

"There's something else too, isn't there?" I asked.

"Yes, I was thinking about my sister. She died when I was four. She was the next younger than I. I used to make her up and carry her around with me like she was some kind of porcelain doll. It was a long time ago. My family is unraveling now that my parents are gone. I am afraid I won't see any of them ever again. Especially now I chose to move away, and I live so far from all of them, but I was suffocating in my hometown. Now I feel so alone."

"There are holidays, and you have your brother with you. And you've got me. Here." I presented the roses still behind my back.

"Oh my, they're gorgeous." Silka gave me a huge kiss. She reached for them, practically a lunge, and put them in a vase with water.

"I guess my timing was good?"

"It always is," my close companion said to me. "But I worry if I really have you," my friend said quickly and then changed the subject. "Let's get some coffee. My treat. We'll take my brother and sit outside. It's not too cold, right?'

"Right, let's go. But I insist on paying. Any man would lay down a treasure for you."

I got an eerie feeling in the parking lot of the bistro. We stepped inside the coffee joint, and there to my left were several men seated in velour crimson-colored highback chairs, wearing fashionable suits and ties and discussing financial opportunities. One man's suit was an Armani; there was no mistaking the cut and the line of the suit, and there were other designer labels in the mix, and it was a curious sight in this coffee shop. They laughed as we came in through the front door. It was a raucous, uncouth laugh, as if they had expected our arrival and just acknowledged a dirty joke about us. I definitely felt they were laughing at me. I caught myself and told myself words a friend had always said to me that I simply was not as important as I thought. It was not said to harm my ego, but simply to quell my fears that everyone made fun of me. Unfortunately, I am as important as I fear that I am. It was not a comfortable realization to stumble upon this bit of information either.

I didn't recognize any of them, the men in their pressed suits, though one did favor my father, as I had last seen him. Baldheaded men with white beards all tend to look somewhat alike to me. It was not unusual for me not to recognize anyone. Everyone more or less knew me or of me, and this brought me great discomfort as well, since so many felt they had the right to jump in my conversations and the trashier members of our fair city would outright begin looking for a brawl upon being seated close to me at another table or just finding themselves in my presence one way or another, and even a fine bistro with expensive coffee and exquisite pastries was not a refuge from them. The endless droves of trash that dwelled in our cosmopolitan city made it such a joy to go out on weekends.

These men in their suits and ties did not appear part of the normal landscape. Telepathically, I said, *Hello*, which is in no way meaning it is a part of or a function of speech, or anything like speaking, but there was no response. I knew it was a game. Subterfuge. Deception. I knew they all heard me. All of them could hear me I was certain, when I spoke telepathically, which is in no way meaning to include telepathy with hearing, but for lack of a better understanding, I must do so. Telepathic communication deals much more with energy and telekinesis and putting forth a tangible thought from one's mind, if he or she is capable, upon the wind for the receiver to grab hold of. I am sure I don't know where they all fly to, but on occasion there is a significant response. So, the point is the men heard me and did not respond which was not a good thing, because I knew immediately they were henchmen of my father's. I boldly stepped around them and strode up to the counter and placed an order for myself and Silka and handed the cashier my debit card. It was early enough in the morning and the mellifluous cashier seemed wide awake as if she had been working for hours already, as she probably had been. Silka grabbed a newspaper too and a juice for her brother. She then turned and walked to the outside deck.

As I was exiting to go sit outside with Silka, one of the men spoke to my mind and said, "Your father is very unhappy with you. We wanted you to know." I could not tell which of the gentlemen it was that offered the words of encouragement, and that, of course, is not to include telepathy with words or symbolic language, as I have explained it deals much more directly with energy from one's mind. It is second nature for me, so it has become difficult to explain, as it truly is a complex phenomena.

"What else is new?" I said. I almost made the mistake of saying it out loud, verbalizing it, which would have been a bit of a conundrum as I was in my own company only, as I said, Silka had gone outside and was waiting for me, but I caught myself. When more voices flooded in, it was more difficult to resist speaking aloud to them. The voices were very cunning and tricky beyond human resort, and I had my hands full with them at times. It is the mark of a mentally ill person under attack, and people are right to be cautious at that time because he or she will do anything to avoid the onslaught. So few understand mental illness, even mostly the mentally ill are unaware of its dynamics. The psychiatrists, particularly if they are Freudian in practice, understand it the least of any population on earth. It is better to allow the hunted ones to wallow in the gutter and not say or do anything for them when engaged in fighting off the voices they apparently hear, and do actually indeed hear. Only the police are brave enough to advance at times like that, and it is their job and a part of which they do not relish because of the unpredictability. A crazed individual, like a large cat in a snare, will do anything and survival of the species is the strongest instinct there is, surpassing the need for procreation in every way at the times it is required.

As we were sitting on the back deck and Silka and I were reading the local newspaper, *The Sentinel*, which was not too terrible of a rag as newspapers went nowadays, something quite odd happened. I heard a woman's voice with a French accent speak directly into a deep recess of my mind. I could not make out who the speaker was, but it was the same voice who had told me to beware the ides of March. Today was March first. It warned me that plenty of trouble was afoot, and I had better "wise up," it had said, and the voice did so with an unpleasant tone, as though I were doing something foolish, and I needed to act in a more mature manner and quit my reckless behavior. Once again I considered it might be my father's voice, but I thought better of it because obviously perilous times were approaching, and this particular voice sought to warn me of impending doom, if I didn't wise up, as the lady's voice commanded. I spoke back to the disembodied voice through my mind and the energy of my mind, but there was no further connection. Silka and I sat there silently reading the newspaper and drinking our coffee. Her brother sat quietly as well. I had bought him another juice and he seemed happy with that. He smiled a lot, and he smiled a lot at me. It made me feel good.

The three of us got up to leave the coffee shop, and we walked back through the lobby and seating area from the back deck and out the front door. "Zing, zing, zing," I heard three shots the moment I stepped onto the sidewalk in front. They grazed my ear I thought, but I was sadly mistaken, and I say sadly for a reason. I had no proof there was a gunman.

"Did you hear that?" I said. My hearing grows quite acute in times of peril.

"No, what?" Silka said.

"Get in the car. There's a sniper. That was a high-powered rifle. They are shooting at us…" My mind trailed off and I could barely believe it had begun. Now Silka was definitely the one. I knew for certain because I was in her presence when it had begun. I had to not only keep her alive, but myself long enough for her to believe in me. Nothing could happen to her or I was doomed.

"A sniper," Silka broke down laughing. "Is he an art critic? Your imagination is showing, Chris." Silka was enjoying the turn of events and I was petrified. I managed to get her into the caddie as well as her brother and drive off in the opposite direction without hearing any more shots. He or she, and I would not rule out a female sniper, would have had to be on the opposite end of the parking lot on the roof of the grocery store most likely, so that way the bullets would go into a dirt embankment and not break any glass, in case the sniper missed. I thought to check out the roof, but I could do that later. I took the long way to our homes. I couldn't be sure I was safe in my apartment any more, or Silka in hers. I would put in police locks for both front doors, like the ones found up north on occasion. They had to be removed from inside the apartment and no one could go through the door if a police lock was in place. I now could not get out of my city. I thought about it, but it would be harder on me if I did leave. It had begun.

I was going to die this month. Dying didn't trouble me so much. Where I might go when I died is what troubled me. Silka would not see a door open in her mind, nor would I be able to hear her, if I was say in a coma. My end played out differently from my father's. In fact, it was nothing like my father's death what I would experience. I dropped Silka off and went to the hardware store to get the police locks, two of them, one for her door and one for mine. It would give me more peace of mind.

"A police lock. Did the apartment management say you could put that on? I don't want it."

"Please, Silka, just indulge me. It's just added protection. All it is, is a piece of metal that prevents the door from being opened from outside and you can't set it in place and lock yourself out."

"I know what it is. Aren't you carrying this joke a little too far?" Really, Christopher, it's enough already. You're starting to scare me a little. Have you been taking your medication? I want to know and tell me the truth."

"This has nothing to do with my medication. It's fine. I take it every day. I was right about the grocery store robbery. Please let me do this so that if there was going to be a problem, there won't be one."

"Okay, put it on," Silka said. "I hope I don't ever need it because of you."

"Thanks a lot, Silka. I'm trying to make sure you don't get caught in a crossfire."

"All right," she said as she dramatically gesticulated her hands. "How long will it take? Have you thought of involving the police?"

"About fifteen minutes. Are you going out? No police," I said.

"Tatianna and I are going shopping. Unless you think there are people at the mall that want to murder me," Silka said.

I couldn't have her live her life from inside an apartment, so I could say nothing or very little. "No, go, go. Have fun. I'm sorry for such a fuss." I sat and thought for a moment as I installed the locking mechanism. *Maybe,* I considered, *it was better if Silka was unaware of what truly was going on. I would not have an ally in this fight, and if I did,* I pondered, *I might lose her and that was not the way it needed to be. It would be the worst solution for both of us.* Then I sat for a longer moment on Silka's living room carpet and asked myself a serious question. It was one with which I had to be honest with myself. *Am I using Silka? I love her even though I have not told her as much. And I need her, and I want her beside me, even with the difficulties I am likely to experience with her there. I don't know. I'll think about it later. But I don't think I am using her.*

Chapter Twelve

The night sky when I turned in was purple. It was not a harbinger of good tidings. The sky was a frightful sign and punishing in the sense I had never seen one like it before and knew it was meant for me. My lockdown was perhaps coming to an end. It was a sign from across the cosmos that my final dance hopefully on earth had begun. I could possibly immigrate to where I was supposed to go, and no longer be struck on a dying planet. Or I might be stuck for another eternity and then what would become of me? I had even less of an idea. It would not be good, so I needed to get while the getting was good. I had no knowledge of the outcome either way—stay or go. I preferred to go. I did not know where I might be going, but it had to be better than life here. I was constantly assured of that. I had only a faint sketch of what I might do to increase my odds of getting out of here and that had been revealed to me, but in bits and pieces. The knowledge of what I could do, or needed done was fairly certain, and I felt it was accurate.

A woman had to see my good nature and fall in love with me. Fall in love with me, not with what I could provide, or my talents or gifts or abilities, but with me as a person. I was lovable enough I felt, but had never had the opportunity to be on the receiving end of a mutual love affair. The women in college mostly loved the sex, as others did, and none were prone to stick around if the weather brought storms, and it inevitably did. They would always talk a good game like they were prepared for anything with me, and it seemed a couple of them were, but my relationships never really lasted. I had married Alison because I owed it to her, after destroying her chances of becoming a mother, which I did not really feel were that significant to her anyway, but I still married her.

Chanel was not the loving, affectionate type, though we remained strong, fierce allies. Chanel was like the sister I wished I had in many ways. We might have been related in a previous life. I would visit her today, and give Silka a little breathing room. Silka and I had dinner plans, so I could go a few hours without seeing her. Silka was not too thrilled with me lately, but there were signs I was telling the truth about my predicament, such as what Tatianna had told her and the grocery store incident. But I was sure Silka wrote them off to coincidence, always a huge underestimation of what in general occurs in the universe. So many of our parts are scripted, and where there is chaos it too occurs in a very orderly fashion. "Life is a stage and we fret our parts."

I had had another notable dream on the heels of the last one. This one involved my sister, Dinah. The final image was quite graphic. She had fastened a belt to her neck and attached it to the rod that held the shower curtain. My shower curtain rod would have just come off the wall, but hers I guess was affixed well, and in this manner she asphyxiated herself. Her face was the color of the purple sky I had seen before I turned in to sleep. I was caught in a quandary. I wanted to help Dinah because I knew she always needed money, but I was afraid I would be financing her drug habit, and then again there was a stern warning from my father's attorney that nothing of what I had should go to my sister, not just the estate I was left, paltry at best as it was, but my own personal accounts as well. It was a difficult matter. We had been friends once upon a time, but not in so long—it seemed we could not remember how or why we had acted friendly toward each other.

I got out of bed and thought whether or not what I saw with my sister in a bathroom somewhere might be true. Had she killed herself already or was she going to? I would not know unless I called her, and I was unlikely to do that. If I did call her, I would not mention the dream. Or perchance she would call me, though she was so angry the last time we spoke, I doubted that might happen either.

I decided instead to go to the park and watch the dogs run and perhaps feed the pigeons and ducks. I had no luck with painting at the moment, so I felt like I did sometimes, quite often actually, as though I was an older retired man, whose hours and days were basically carefree and meaningless. I had outlived my usefulness and all my friends, and I was basically a part of something that no longer existed. My days were neither, however, but I could not escape the feeling that I was a retired older gent with nothing to do and no one to do it with. So I grabbed some bread and went out to my car. The ducks would appreciate me at least.

I did not make a huge sum annually from selling my paintings, and I had to produce to make that, as it was a tough business selling fine art, but I had shows often, and here and there were warm receptions that found me and to which I was invited, and I had made a big splash in Los Angeles recently for some reason. It was not even six figures I earned annually, but near that, so all in all not a bad chunk of money, but to support myself this way was the true prize. So very few artists are able. Chicago had been kind to me as well in recent months. With the insurance money I could actually afford to take some time off, but what was coming would be no vacation. Believe it or not, it had temporarily slipped my mind. When I regained some form of conscious thought as to my situation, I felt sure this was the last month of my life. I might not paint again, or then I might. Inspiration was largely chemical, as I have said, and passion dies hard.

I wound up sitting on a bench at the park where an older man joined me. He was bald and had a white beard and was wearing a denim jacket and a golfer's cap. We never spoke and there was an obvious tension between us. I fed the pigeons and pitched little bits of bread into the pond, so the turtles could eat as well. This elderly gentleman, obviously of some means it would appear was driving a BMW and seemed to be sucking the energy right out of me. It felt like my medication was peaking, as I would get hot flashes often when it did, but I had not taken my morning meds yet. It had to be this older man, sucking the very life force out of my bones and blood.

I got up to leave and he cleared his throat as if he was going to say something, and then perhaps he thought better of it, or never intended to and was just clearing his throat after all. It did not seem significant enough to me either way, but I noticed it. I was finely attuned to my surroundings. I knew bad things were going to start happening and I dreaded my existence. So, I got in my car and drove a bit. Where the park was, was a beautiful neighborhood with old ivy-laden two-story brick homes with white picket fences. The entire neighborhood just about was like that. They were dream homes, but had gotten so old now that I am sure the upkeep was a nightmare.

As I motored along down various mean streets and back roads, I heard my mother's voice. "He can't do it unless you let him." That was what the voice I heard in my mind said. It was clearly my mother's voice, and though I did not try to communicate with her, I knew she was trying to help me. The "he" referred to had to be my father and what he was incapable of doing I was not so sure. It was proof enough that there was going to be some action taken against my will, and I had the power to stop the act right in its tracks. Just then a squirrel ran across my path and I jammed on my brakes.

I found myself in some bit of discomfort, not mentally, but physically as my side began to hurt. I had pulled a muscle in my right hip, making love to Silka. I felt so old and useless this morning. I could not get anything right. Everything was barricaded or walled off from me, even simple movements such as bending down and picking up something from the ground were painful. It occurred to me I was aging, and rapidly, but there was no change in my physical appearance that I could tell. I was growing older though. The process felt fairly definite to me. My mind as well was becoming more muddled. It had not seemed so clear to me, but I decided it was true.

The trees Chris noticed looked unnatural. They were bent and stooped like trees that were hundreds of years old. The moss drizzled from them. I got out of my car and examined an old oak. Its branches were nearly touching the ground and the shady area it provided looked dark and menacing. Then it happened. All the creatures around me began to communicate with me. The squirrels, the lizards, the birds all had two cents to chime in. The voices in my head were deafening. They quoted catechisms, aphorisms and adages. "A penny found is a penny saved, my boy." The black birds chirped from the power line above. Or little insignificant facts would come my way from my new friends. "Coffee and textiles are the chief exports of Guatemala." Or, "Go ahead, you know you want to." These sayings would cleverly coincide with something I was thinking about. I wanted to break off a flower from a magnolia tree, when the last saying of *my wanting to do it* rang like a chime in my head. If I had taught myself anything over the years it was to resist the voices. Some are helpful, but mostly very many of them are not, and I could easily get into trouble if I paid attention. So now I assumed the battle was on, and the first prize would be my sanity. The voices would beat me down till I was uncertain of what I was doing. I had never succeeded when it had gotten this bad before. And then there was Silka. I would have to avoid her somehow for a time. That was a depressing reality.

Chapter Thirteen

To his credit, Chris stood his ground. He would not be bowled over by the voices in his head, but he wondered how he would sleep or have dinner with Silka. He could stay up through the night, but he would have to cancel his dinner engagement. Extraneous conversation accompanied by the voices in his head would be too much for a dinner date.

He returned to his apartment and checked his answering machine. There was already a message from Silka saying she had to cancel, and that she was going away for a week or so, but would be back on Sunday night and would come over then. Sunday would be the tenth of March. So as Chris expected, his only ally in his fight had been bought off or turned away from him somehow, and he naturally assumed the guilt for having done it himself. But whatever happened, he would have had to do something similar, so this was not bad happenstance. He would have had to protect Silka some way, so her going away for a week was not a stroke of good luck.

The voices were not quieted fully since he had come indoors, but mostly they were at the moment. He decided he would channel the energy and paint, so he went into his studio and stayed there until five hours after sundown and barely took anything to eat or drink but water and one sandwich, while he waited for the piece he was working on to dry in places. It was the piece of him and Silka and he now wanted to finish it and give it to her. He had taken his revolver into his studio with him. He turned in to sleep, but could not and wound up tossing and turning all night. Even though nearly finishing the painting had made him feel better, he could not think of anything but Silka and whether cancelling dinner plans was such a good idea, even though she apparently had the same idea. He would bring her coffee in the morning.

During the time Chris had been out the previous day, another scene with Silka had unfolded simultaneously that would have significant consequences for the two of them.

Silka was in a hurry to meet Tatianna for lunch. She grabbed her keys and brushed on make-up in the car. She was meeting Tatianna uptown at a small bar and grill that was known for serving delicious sandwiches and salads. Silka had a rule about such places. If it was an entirely trendy spot, it usually meant it was noisy, and she had gotten used to quiet dinners with Chris and no longer tolerated the hubbub and din of people's conversations as well. She wondered if this was a characteristic she now shared with Chris. It must obviously be so, she considered. She knew he was mentally ill, and as a couple, she did not wish to grow like him in that regard. His disease was very degenerative. Every time he had an episode, Silka understood, it would be worse than the one before. Artists shared their misery in connection with one another. Another troubled artist is the only consolation and with whom only one that is a troubled artist can commiserate. Silka wondered what she could really do for Chris. If he would stay, she would try to make him happy. She had so many relationships cut short, it was difficult for her to consider undertaking another one that had those possible earmarks.

There was a man seated with Tatianna. Silka noticed him immediately as she walked in and she did not know him, but wondered if it was the infamous Jude that Silka had heard so much about. Her suspicions proved to be correct. Tatianna was smiling, laughing, and did not appear the least bit frightened by him, as she introduced her partner. Silka had thought the pair had broken up. That seemed like an obvious outcome to Silka.

"So you are the notorious Jude I have heard so much about. Chris barely goes a day without mentioning some plot you have against him," Silka said.

"It's not what you think. I was just explaining to Tatianna that she had confused my comments about Chris. I never dreamed of killing him. She told me of your meeting. I was extremely upset with Chris and have been for years, but I want to put petty differences aside. I have no proof he did what I thought he did. The marriage was on its last legs anyway. If he did that to my wife, then he'll have to answer for it. I now have no wish to harm Chris. I want to help him, but my big fear is for the both of you, particularly you, Silka. I have my ears to the ground in this town, Silka. I know a lot that goes on here. I had no idea how bad things were getting for Chris. I now really want to help him. Call it sentimentality. I am ready to settle up with the pain and embarrassment he has caused me over the years and just let bygones be bygones, but I can't forget about him. My worry as I stated is for the two of you. Chanel is an evil bitch. She'll get hers. She's probably egging him on.

"Egging him on at what?" Silka asked. She grew a little defensive. Jude had no right to talk about these people that way. It was his first time meeting her too. He was a bold, impudent man, and he lacked the class of her lover.

"He's losing his mind is what I have heard. And Chanel wants to cheat him on his insurance money, so that he does not even know he's been cheated."

"How do you know details like this? Did you tell him that Tatianna?" Silka asked.

"Chris came into the gallery today and threatened Chanel about something," Tatianna said. "I could only hear a little, but it didn't sound pleasant. And then he left in a huff and she went into the bathroom and cried. They were both quite agitated, but like I said I could not hear everything clearly.

"It could have been about anything." Silka said. "It could have been about his mom. He and Chanel have been friends forever. Why do you assume he threatened her? They love each other as near as I can tell. And she makes him a lot of money."

"Here's what I wish would happen. I want the two of you to stay in my ranch house in Lake Buena Vista. You'll be safe there. And no, I'm not going to involve the police. There's nothing they can do at this point. Take my word for that. Just get away with Tatianna. Try it for a week."

"I've got my brother. I don't like just moving Hinton around like that."

"I know," Jude said. "But it's a three bedroom. There's a video game console in the living room too. He'll be comfortable."

"What do I tell Chris? That is assuming I decide I am in danger, which the suggestion of it spooks me a little bit. About you, Jude, not as much about Chris. When someone is in danger your name seems to get mentioned as well."

"I know. I know you have no reason to trust me. I'm just trying to do what is right. I'm not the monster Chris paints me. I'll stay away from the ranch house. Just the three of you use it. Tell Chris you're needed elsewhere and you have arranged some time off...you know...it's family business. He'll never know. I promise."

In this manner, Jude could effectively kidnap both women, and they would never know they had been kidnapped. And he could keep them both under wrap so neither of them could assist Chris. He was playing on their innate sense of trust as younger less experienced women than he, a vicious man who had played these games all his life, and the fact that he was a master manipulator. And he knew his pro hitters were in town, so it would be over soon. He even knew there had been a failed attempt, though the hitters were not associating or communicating with Jude. He was out of the picture, and that suited Jude fine. It was exactly what he wanted.

He was also effectively excluding himself from the picture by setting up alibis for the two young ladies. If he knew when the hit was going to be, he could spend the night at his ranch house he had so graciously offered the services of, with Tatianna and then have an iron-clad alibi. Even though he had lied and said he wouldn't, he planned to do just that, and he felt certain he would get wind of when the hit was coming. Chris knew nothing of the ides of March, however, which the specific date being March fifteenth, when Brutus and others stabbed Caesar in the theatre of Pompey. The day of the lunch meeting was only March second. Even if Silka did agree and could not go immediately, one week would put her return to her apartment short of the fifteenth. All great plans have too many variables to control.

After lunch, Silka went back to the gallery with Tatianna, and said to her, "I'm thinking about Jude's offer. He seems reasonable, but I'm not sure I would trust him too much, Tatianna."

"I know. He's a bit of a schemer. But a week at his house in Lake Buena Vista would be nice. I'll try to get him to throw in theme park tickets. It's a cool house. He took me there on our first date," Tatianna said.

Silka was really thinking and concentrating on something else. "You see. The problem is I have a good job now, except for the hours. My kid brother is home by himself too much in the evenings. That's not good for him and I worry about him. He is in a special needs program during the day, but they close at five. I need a regular nine to five. And something close by. Do you know of anything?"

"No, but I'll keep my ears open. I can leave early today. Susan is here and Chanel left. I don't know what happened between her and Chris. They are almost always laughing when they are together. I'll find out and let you know. That way you don't have to ask Chris. If you want me to."

"Okay, thanks. I've got to get ready for work. I'll see you later."

Chris needed to see his doctor, and as it was now the next day, he figured the good-looking receptionist would be able to fit him in on a Friday without too much trouble. Chris seriously doubted his doctor could do anything for him, but Chris could at least try to get him to do something that might prove beneficial for his patient. The receptionist gave him an appointment for the afternoon. Chris had managed to drag himself out of bed, but he could not face showering. It simply was impossible some days in times like these. He had gotten coffee for himself and Silka, but found she did not open her door. Her music was off, so Chris assumed she had pulled a morning shift or possibly had left already to wherever she was going.

He arrived at his doctor's office, a Lanham A. Benjamin MD, a board-certified psychiatrist, a half an hour early. The waiting room was tiny and crowded. There were several faux French Impressionist paintings adorning the walls of the waiting room to give off that cheap but elegant ambience. Chris sat down next to a couple. The woman looked considerably younger than the man she sat next to, but she had a hard face like she had had a tough life or spent years in the sun. Chris heard her make reference to the man sitting next to her as her husband during a cell phone conversation. Chris' voices were a little more subdued. He flipped through a magazine. Chris considered she was the patient, but when the name Robert was called the man got up and walked past the receptionist's desk down a narrow hallway, and his wife remained seated. The man had a limp and Chris could tell his right ankle hurt him terribly. Chris could feel the pain of the man's stress fracture in his right ankle.

Then it was Chris' turn to see his psychiatrist. The other patients waiting were there probably to see other counselors or therapists because they had arrived earlier than Chris and he was actually the next to go in. They might have had later appointments than Chris, but he doubted that since he had arrived so early for his appointment.

"Doctor Benjamin, I'm not doing so well. I keep having panic attacks and feel like I am going to die, and I hate to say this, but I think someone is trying to kill me. There were shots at a coffee shop I frequent from across the street and I think the guy was aiming for me."

Doctor Benjamin rarely looked up from his laptop that he took patients' notes on. Chris always joked with him that he was playing the latest video game, but his doctor never saw the humor in it. But this time was different. Chris was in a serious mood and he needed help. From somewhere, anywhere. Desperation was seeping in and Chris knew it was likely the doctor couldn't help.

"Why do you think you're a target?" the psychiatrist asked.

"It's the voices I've been hearing. Is there something I'm not doing that I can do and block them out more fully."

"We might need to consider changing your meds. I think I am going to order an anti-depressant for you too. How have you been sleeping?"

"Not very well," Chris said.

"This should help."

It was only a fifteen-minute appointment and the doctor never once glanced at Chris until he got up. He transcribed notes into his laptop and then printed the prescriptions. Then the doctor said, "Two weeks. We'll see how you do on your new meds." The doctor stood up and opened the door to his office, shook Chris' hand and said, "Feel better."

Chris was certain he would be dead within two weeks. It was the third of March. Chris decided it didn't really matter if he had the prescriptions filled or not, but then a change in meds might make his life easier, or tougher, depending on how the change went. Chris was leery of anti-depressants. He did not tolerate them well and had a huge problem when on an anti-depressant once before. But he decided as well, he would give it another try. If he was going to die, and soon, it didn't really matter. Chris understood insanity; he had lived with it most of his life. Chris realized, in fact, that he could do almost anything, as long as he remained out of prison, as there had to be greater accessibility to his person, if he was going to be murdered. But then, of course, he could be murdered in prison just as easily, but the food would be substantially better if he stayed out. Those decisions might have already been made by someone with more clout than Chris in such matters.

Chris went back to his apartment and finished the painting he was working on. It needed to dry overnight and then at some opportune moment he could present it to Silka. *A parting gift*, Chris mused.

Chapter Fourteen

Chris considered it was better to be farsighted than nearsighted. He was losing some vision close at hand, but his acuity for greater distances had gotten better. It seemed natural enough at his age, but there was more to it. He could be attacked by someone or something coming at him from a distance, but if he was attacked from nearby or at close range, *mano a mano*, his natural defensive measures would kick in more precisely and more spontaneously. If the attack was sudden on his person, he could make a sudden reaction, more so than if it came at him from a distance. That seemed natural to Chris too. But his senses were what were under attack. His perception grew cloudier each day.

He had gone to get a sandwich at a local eatery, and through the glass he had seen a woman look at him before he entered. Her face looked very contorted. Her ears were longer and her chin was longer and her eyes looked misshapen and uneven, and Chris knew he was seeing her for real, and wondered if she even knew this was how she presented herself. Probably she did not, Chris concluded, or she might not find herself in public if she was aware of her true appearance, but then Chris wondered how many saw her as she really was.

She had "unlocked" her true appearance in front of Chris, which was usually a sign to stay away. It might just be him, Chris wondered; he had not seen this sort of thing often, or she might have some control over when she faded in and out of her true looks. She appeared a moment later to be a good-looking gal, and Chris waited behind her in line, and though he knew fully what he had seen, he had to appear as though he was not afraid. She might go for his juggler if she smelled fear. More likely, she would leave him alone because he had been marked and she knew Chris was being followed. She knew his time was drawing near and she planned not to offer help or her services. If engaged in conversation, which Chris was not going to do, the woman would be polite, perhaps even generous, as it is not so hard to be to a dying man.

So an attack that was sudden or of a surprise nature was easier to ward off, because Chris' senses would kick in that much faster. If it was premeditated and came down the road from him, particularly if it picked up steam, Chris tended to tense up and feel uncomfortable and could end up defenseless. He had seen Chanel "unlock" several times before, but only into a more gorgeous creature. And Chanel was quite good looking on a bad day. It was always after making love that Chanel chose to "unlock" her true looks, and it was always to keep Chris in bed longer, and it always worked. He had never seen her demonic side and did not wish to.

"I would count the minutes until we meet again," Chris heard the voice say in his mind. It was Jude's voice.

"It's all a mistake, Jude. You are not who you think you are. Let me be," Chris answered out loud. He was walking away from the sandwich shop. He had sat on the covered patio and eaten his sandwich and was now moving toward his car.

"You expect me to believe that?" The sound of distant sirens clashed with the quiet in the parking lot. Chris opened his car door. Just then, a grisly looking man stepped from around the back of a mini-van and said, "Give me your money. Now asshole." He was brandishing a semi-automatic pistol. "Now," he screamed. He pointed the gun at Chris' heart and was about to squeeze the trigger when Chris by reflex knocked the gun away from his heart and out of the man's hand. A shot was fired and the police officer parked at the other end of the parking lot heard the gun go off. The man ran back to his car parked nearby, a beaten-up-looking Chevy. The officer followed him and a chase was underway. Chris pulled out and went in the opposite direction. He did not want any involvement with the police. One or more of them were likely to get hurt, and they had done nothing to Chris. This was between Jude, Chris and his father.

"I can't believe your luck, buddy boy." Chris' father's voice rang clear this time. It was amidst the din and chatter of the other voices in his mind. It was not one of his father's henchmen or one of the pro hitters just then. The attempt at robbery and mayhem was Dinah's boyfriend, and now he would be locked up. Possession of a firearm, resisting arrest, attempted murder, reckless driving. He was off the street, and Dinah would probably be sent to prison as his accomplice, whether the police knew Chris was involved or not. The police would be in touch with him most likely though. Chris was not dropping by the police station, however. No formal complaints from Chris. Now was not the time. They could figure it out on their own or find him. By the time Dinah's boyfriend saw a judge it would be after the fifteenth, so Chris did not have to worry about him. Nor would he worry about Dinah either. She might not even be alive. He went home and took his anti-depressant, hoping it would make him groggy and he could sleep.

Chris did sleep and no sooner than he had drifted off, he heard the sound of breaking glass again. He thought to call 911, but then called out, "children," from his bedroom. It was accompanied by the sound of laughter and then what sounded like a television tube being blown out. Chris had to get up. It would be fun to watch them play, though at best, his twins were shadowy figures and he could not see them well. They might have their light sabers out, however.

But they did not have their light sabers. Chris was oddly disappointed in a way. They had some type of cap pistol it sounded like, and upon impact, the guns, which were not exactly toys, made a huge explosion. They were wrecking Chris' apartment obviously, but there was no actual damage done. His twins were somehow parallel a reality or two. "Oh, good one," Chris said when the stereo went up in flames. Chris could spot a flash of light hitting an object in his living room. The object would come aglow with a green light and then disappear momentarily, but, of course, it remained in place and did not actually disappear. He encouraged them to have their fun, and then something happened that had never happened before. In unison, they both spoke to Chris and said, "We love you, daddy." Chris nearly cried. He certainly grew misty. "I love you both as well." And that was followed by more laughter and two simultaneous "booms" from either end of the living room. "Are you going to let daddy sleep?" There was no answer, but the room was quiet, and Chris went back to bed.

Chris had noticed something else when he was out, not just the unnatural look of the trees. The power lines, of which there were plenty that streamed alongside every road and intersection in Orlando, had menacing little flashes of shadow that crept by as Chris drove under them. He felt like the electric lines were humming as well. He could feel it in his inner ears. And he felt trapped by them, constricted somehow. Chris would feel all hot and flushed as well, and it did not matter whether he had taken his medication or not, which lately he was forgetting to take. He was too far gone for it to make much of a difference now. The power lines signified areas that were little prisons guarded and walled off with electrical current. Never before had Chris noticed such a thing.

The gleam of light from a puddle in the road took on all new meaning and was very newly disturbing to Chris. When he might have been tempted to splash through a roadside puddle with his car, now he found he was avoiding them as though they were some sort of trap he could not see the bottom of. But the electric lines were worse. He now discovered they were everywhere he went. He had never truly noticed them before. They guarded every business, every house, every sidewalk, and the electric authority kept putting up more and more each year. Chris had not thought about it before, but then he realized what else he had seen. There were all these electrified birds on the wires of the electric and telephone poles. They looked like they had been fried. It was haunting and grotesque at the same time.

Certainly, the planet was baking itself. It was not just from the upper atmosphere and the lack of ozone, but right down on the ground too. Everyone was imprisoned and being cooked. Chris' end was sooner than the demise of the planet and he was beginning to believe that was a merciful circumstance, but not long after he would leave, and he still had little idea of where to that might be; he felt the planet would implode and be an unlivable, dead rock. Earth would be a footnote in the universe. The birds had seemed to hover around like buzzards do, circling, circling, waiting and watching. They were looking for food and though they were not carrion eaters, they seemed hungry, and sometimes as he drove along, they would call out to him. "Chris, Chris, where you going? Take me with you, Chris. A humming bird eats one-eighth of its weight daily, Chris. Chris we know who you are. Won't you talk to us?" Even the dead fried birds on the wires would call out to him. "Help us, Chris. Chris, we need your help." It became difficult, nearly impossible to go out, so Chris spent more time at home.

He knew, however, if he was truly going to be murdered, he would have to get out more often and walk among the people. His coffee shop was nearby. He could park the car for a little while, but that seemed unlikely that he would. There was also a grocery store nearby. Getting to the bank would be a little tricky, but he had credit cards, and now was as good of a time as any to use them. He might even do some shopping if he felt better. He had maybe ten days left on earth…that called for a celebration. But then, there had already been a fair bit of excitement lately.

"He wants us both, son. Fight for me." The voice was of Chris' mother.

"I will," Chris said out loud. He did not know if she could hear him. "I'll fight."

There was a knock at the door of his apartment. Chris opened it. His revolver lay in the bedroom.

"Maintenance. I've got to change the air filter. It's in your ceiling."

Chris had seen the portal to the attic, and wondered what was up there. He always looked to see if any insulation was on the carpet, when he came in. If insulation had dropped from the portal down to the carpet, it meant someone was up there, but it had never been so. The maintenance man's timing seemed creepy, but Chris tolerated his presence in his home the best he could, and turned on the television in the living room to watch some of the financial news, but he could not pay attention well. Chris was falling apart. He was not sure though. He was no longer sure what was real and what was bleeding through from some alternative reality.

"Ok. Got it. That should fix you up. It might lower your electric bills too."

"Thank you very much." Chris found the gentleman comforting in a strange way. Yes, he decided he needed help, and this man had helped him, and that was what he needed. But Chris would not check into a hospital. They are death traps and the scariest things go on in hospitals. So, he was essentially stuck. He had no one to turn to, until Silka got back. He could not read, nor watch television comfortably, sleeping was a problem…Chris was stuck, a prisoner of his mind and body. So he decided to pack up. He would go somewhere for the remaining days Silka was out.

As Chris did not pay much attention to the local news, he did not know that a certain road out of town was closed for maintenance. It was a way he was familiar with and liked because it put him on the edge of town quickly. Chris thought he might drive to New Orleans or Austin, Texas. The purpose was the drive, not really to sightsee or visit anyone, but as he pulled out on his main artery out of town, it was closed and he grew upset and suspicious.

He turned around and went down another street less known to him, which took him past these horribly Gothic-looking buildings downtown. The buildings were monstrous looking, with windows bricked in or pale crosses drawn to section them off, and imposing, sweeping turrets with fair damsels trapped inside, and Chris could imagine where the gargoyles would go. He knew his way around most of downtown, but none of this part looked like anything he had ever seen, and everything seemed so eerie and tense.

He could see little scenes and acts and people and incidental dramas, inside of deserted buildings, where no person should or could be. They dotted the open parts of the infrastructure, whereby Chris could look in and see what was going on. But what Chris saw were not people, and he was aware of this reality. Parking garages were firing their lights at Chris. Every stream of light was a shot of pain inflicted on Chris. They shot him endlessly as he drove by, and the traffic lights would not cooperate. He was stuck under enemy fire, mesmerized into standing still, even when the light had changed to green. There was no one on the street and in his mind he witnessed what looked like burned out buildings as if war had been declared and a missile strike had taken place in his hometown. Broken glass glittered in the streets. Cars were on blocks, their tires harvested and parts cannibalized. He understood he was not actually traveling through his city. It was another part of the universe and it seemed like a deep pit of Hell.

Then as he sped up at the merge and climbed on I-4 going out of town, a voice said, "They're after you," and all Chris could witness was that he was surrounded by black SUVs. He had merged right into a dozen black SUVs. The drivers were all men in business suits, young, goodlooking, fortyish and tanned. They all smiled at him one by one as he drove by. He had to get away. He could not travel in that pack. They would run him off the road or squeeze him into a guardrail or concrete abutment. He crossed over the interstate between a half-dozen traffic cones, driving perilously and almost blind down the wrong side of I-4, dodging cars and certain mayhem and death, running the other drivers coming toward him off the road. He slipped to the inside lane and was driving alongside the guardrail, where people parked their cars briefly if they had engine trouble, but his caddie stuck out into the next lane that traveled east as he was going west. Horns blared, people waved him off as they dodged him, and then he heard a voice; it was actually two voices. "Take the next exit, daddy." His twins were bailing him out. He cut a sharp left across three lanes of traffic and took the exit and got off the interstate and headed out of town. It was perhaps the most harrowing moment of all this that Chris had endured and experienced, and five minutes later he was fine, driving along, and he turned on the CD player in his car, and had forgotten about everything that just happened.

He was free and no one was after him and he had the road out of town all to himself. There was traffic separated by a concrete medium going into town, but none leaving, except Chris. But it felt to Chris like he was developing a high blood pressure problem, and he could actually feel it, but he thought how senseless it would be to take even more medication. He would enjoy his few days and nights of driving and return under cloak of darkness and then go get coffee and lunch and dinner on the fifteenth of March. That was his plan. He would dictate the terms now. It was all going to be his call. He felt like a king on the open road. He imagined universes inside of universes and he thought about his diamonds. The ones he had rescued from his safe, and had been in the evil clutches of his wife, but she had never figured that one out.

He would give the diamonds to Silka. What woman would turn down the gift? He would bribe Silka to get coffee with him on the fifteenth with a quarter million dollars in first-cut diamonds. Or no, he would give them to her afterwards, before dinner. Or wait. Would she think he was proposing? He was uncertain. He could not get married for obvious reasons. He was not divorced yet, and he had only known Silka a couple of months. It would be one final farewell in his current form and a good meal and then he would be allowed to exit. Chris longed to die in his sleep. He was sick of his sickness and the high drama. He knew whatever happened now, he was not staying here. He was going away, away from this planet, and Chris felt great about it. He felt like two million bucks.

What if he could take Silka with him? What if he actually came back and grabbed her and they made the exodus to where he was going. The place was appointed by now, Chris felt relatively sure. Silka always claimed she had abandonment issues, what with her parents, and the farm, and her brother, and the sister that died, and if Chris could persuade her she could come with him. It would be a better world for sure, and he might have twins. They might have the twins in their next lives.

Chris drove on. He hooked up with I-75 going north, which had plenty of traffic but was a good road up the middle of the state and to the north and south, and he could drop off here and there and catch other state roads that gave a more direct route to where he was going. He was driving by the air base in Pensacola, and so many of the enlisted came out to see him. They drove from exit to exit, saluting him as he drove by. They chattered on their CB radios, "It's Chris. He came. Hey, Chris. We love you, man." Chris waved and drove on toward New Orleans. If he remembered correctly it was I-610 that went around New Orleans so he would not be stuck in so much traffic, and Chris was correct and he took it, but he needed to stop for gas. He barely ate a thing anymore and had started to drop weight, but was feeling better as a result. He pulled off the interstate to get gas and got lost trying to get back on and wound up near the levees around midnight. They were not high walls at all, Chris noticed, what were left of them. There were also huge holes in some of them. And New Orleans is below sea level by several feet.

Chris was confused how to get back on the interstate and a black man at a gas pump said telepathically, *follow that car*, and Chris did, and he got right back on the interstate. People are friendly here he decided, but he would not take any unnecessary chances. His revolver was in the glove compartment. Out-of-state license plates are always a dead giveaway. Too many people prey upon those with out-of-state license plates. Chris drove off in the direction of Texas. He was feeling good. The air was crisp at night, and he drove along with his CD player on, the windows down and the heater warming his feet. Finally, he had had a good idea to get away from his city. What a relief.

Chris started to imagine his new universe more and more, or perhaps it was just a different reality and another planet. There would be those that worked and those that were the royal family that were supported by their own efforts and by that of those who worked. And Chris would be higher up the food chain than he was on earth, and the notion of mental illness, and all that mental illness denoted and connoted would not exist. Good and evil would exist, as the members of the new planet or solar system, or possibly he would find himself in a new galaxy, would of necessity probably have to defend themselves on occasion. And Chris would have a wife or some reasonable facsimile thereof and children, or however that was constituted, and a family that he loved and that loved him. Chris might become a different species or entity altogether. He hoped so. Man was such a delicate creature. Men are weak and break down easily.

Chris pressed on toward Texas, but it was getting time to turn in for the night and get off the road. He found a Quality Inn and got a room. He had a decent night's sleep after watching the Discovery Channel and ordering room service, which was delivered to his room by way of a local Italian place across the road. He had decided to turn back the next day, and not go to Texas after all, but rather to return to Orlando. He felt rejuvenated overnight. It would be nice to return home he decided. Maybe he could resume painting. It was all that mattered in his life, besides Silka. Everything had slipped away from Chris. All the tension, the stress, the nervousness had all evaporated. Chris even took a tub bath. But the fifteenth was approaching.

Just outside of Orlando, Chris was diverted from his path by voices he obeyed. They were coming from a black SUV, and the driver, a man, was chatting on a cell phone, and he told Chris where Chris was going next, and to come take a look. Chris thought it was all over. He thought he would glimpse his next life or the part of the universe or at least surely the planet he would be on soon. But instead, the driver of the SUV took him past a cemetery, and announced "Your new home," and then laughed and drove off. Nothing had changed, and they already knew Chris was back in town. It would be more difficult to escape the next time if Chris chose to. He might just ride it out from here.

Meanwhile, Silka and Tatianna enjoyed their new digs in the lap of luxury. The house had a lake view, sliding glass doors and an outside deck on the back of the house that was just beyond the newly refurbished kitchen inside. The ladies made drinks and settled right in. Silka's brother wasted no time in operating the Playstation. Tatianna had gotten Jude to throw in theme park tickets and the two young women drank, and ate, and played and spoke of old flames and romance and silly stories to amuse each other. But Silka kept coming back to Chris in her conversations with Tatianna. She was uptight and afraid she had wronged him and deserted him by taking some time off from their relationship, which was what she was doing, but had had the grace not to explain it that way to Chris. Tatianna said he would be waiting when she got back.

"He's just so lonely. He doesn't reach out to anyone. It's like he's British or something," Silka said. "The stiff upper lip thing. He's never satisfied with anything he's done, and God help you if you catch him on a day when he can't paint. He walks around aimlessly and bumps into walls and talks to himself. But when he has a good day, he's thoughtful, kind, generous. And he's great with Hinton."

"I had a boyfriend once that was a writer. He never finished one manuscript. He never had anything to show for all those hours, but he was brilliant. But not very good in bed."

"Most men aren't, I have found. If you can train them, it helps."

"I agree. Tell the guy what you like and he does it. It's that simple. And none of this six month, I'm tired of giving massages or foot rubs. Just do what I like. I think men get bored easily because they're so dumb. I really don't like men all that well, but I don't like sex with women," Tatianna said. "It's not for me, whether she looks like a bull mastiff or not."

"Men need one thing and need to do another thing," Silka said. "He has to have money, at least some."

"And what does he have to do?" Tatianna asked.

"He has to tell his family about you. Chris doesn't really have any family to speak of. He says his father was Satan, and he just passed away, and his mother is in an insane asylum and his sister is a drug addict. I think he lost a brother too. So, I don't have to worry about him telling his family. I'll tell my family if the right time comes up."

"Do you really think that is so important?"

"Absolutely, I do. If he doesn't tell a family member or all of them, he's not really serious," Silka said.

The young ladies were becoming friends, and Silka trusted Tatianna to a large extent, and her opinion of Jude had changed. Apparently, she let creep into her consciousness, this had all been a huge misunderstanding from the beginning and for how long before Silka ever met Chris, this had been going on, she did not know or care at this point. Chris was a great man, and she would either simply be with him or without him, and Silka was not going to debate endlessly in her mind which was the more likely outcome. What she told herself was that, but she knew she would probably dissect it over and over. Was Chris the one? And could she trust him?

They curled up in Adirondack chairs and watched the sun go down and made a fresh pitcher of margaritas. They had both needed a vacation it seemed.

After arriving at his apartment, Chris turned in and had a fitful night's sleep. He would toss this way and turn that way, and his shorts rode up on him, and he would kick off the blanket and then pull it right back on again. This dance went on all night. He got out of bed just before sun-up and fixed a cup of coffee and went into his studio. He wanted to sniff the aroma of the work he had completed a couple of days prior. It was easily dry and he would give it to Silka soon. He was pleased with it. The man had a wry, understated smile though the woman had a look of consternation, and a slightly more pained expression as though there was some heartache involved in the matter that had them facing out opposite windows in different parts of a room. The sky outside the windows of the room was the same purple he had seen in his dream, and the walls of the room were white and the woman was dressed in a fashionable yellow shirt with white shorts and the man in brown shorts and a lighter top. It was curious the expressions on their faces. Chris could no longer remember what had inspired him to paint this particular rendering of the scene in his mind.

Chris decided to walk the quarter mile to get another cup of coffee. As he climbed down the stairs and wound up on the street, a parked car, a blue sedan, flashed on its lights and sped down the part of the road where Chris was walking on the sidewalk. The car came careening over the gutter and the curb and took a clear swipe at Chris, but a nimbler Chris ducked behind a concrete telephone pole, and the car turned quickly and sped off, missing the pole by inches. It was early, and no cops had been near the scene, and Chris laughed a little that another attempt had fallen by the wayside. He was in charge. "Thank you, Mademoiselle Blancheflor, wherever you are," Chris said out loud. "I'm in charge. I'm the stronger now. Mom, it will be all right." But there was no answer in his mind or ears. Chris didn't care. It was all real, and it was all coming together.

Chris was the son of Satan, and Satan had been deposed, and now Chris was the stronger, but it was a title he would gladly relinquish back to his father in a few days, if Chris found himself bound for glory on a new star. Chris found the anti-depressant might be working favorably. His knees did not ache so much, and his mind was a little more focused, he thought, but then he still was not sleeping well, but then when had he, he considered? The car looked familiar too. Chris was sure he had seen it parked in his own driveway at his old house with his soon-to-be ex-wife. It was her lover's car. Chris laughed even louder. "I'll fix them all," he muttered and continued to laugh.

Chapter Fifteen

The time had come for me to sign my divorce papers. Alison got the house and in doing so I got out of alimony. She used my attorney so she would not have to pay for one. I had always said she a very cunning woman, but not a smart one. Reggie Tate, my lawyer, basically rubber stamped everything I wanted, because he knew where his check was coming from, and for both parties. He was happy he met me.

Alison did not show up to the proceedings, which was a good thing for me. No last battle, no last scene—I could leave and be done with the albatross for good. Reggie got me in and out quickly as he had promised, and I felt like celebrating. Services rendered. Like every man who can afford to after escaping prison with his life, he wants to buy something nice, something meaningful that is his own. I had decided on a new watch, a Rolex, diamond encrusted. I knew almost nothing about them. I didn't go in for fancy items for myself too much, but I thought I would pick one up at the mall. The notion appealed to me immensely. I left the judge's chambers whistling a tune, "There Must Be Fifty Ways to Park the Hummer."

Silka would return later today. It was a further reason to be in a good mood. Divorced, a new watch and a chance to see my favorite gal, my only gal, my only friend, other than Chanel: the day had glorious written all over it. I headed in the direction of the Mall at Millennia to find Tiffany and Company and see what kind of time pieces they had. I would splurge some hard-earned cash, but my limit was five thousand. Normally, I would never do such a thing for myself, but given the circumstances, why the Hell not? I had won the fight. The voices were quiet. Gone, I thought. Vanquished. My mind was finally at peace. I could think: I could go anywhere and do anything I wanted. I had won.

I arrived at the Mall at Millennia and there was not an SUV in sight. I supposed my father's henchmen were a little scared of me by now, but there being so many of them, I would not test that theory. It was still a time to act prudently and rationally. I walked in by Neiman Marcus and the mall already at noon was a sea of shoppers. Obese ducks, pushing baby strollers and wearing shorts that clung to their behinds, were carrying bags of goodies half-priced as they waddled by me. They quacked at their children incessantly. And then the voices started. "Shit," I muttered under my breath. Nothing had been decided. It was all a sham. I had won nothing. The battle still raged.

One lady walked by and blinked into my brain, "Hi Chris. Victoria's Secret is having a sale. Wouldn't Silka like something nice?"

"Chris good to see you man, where have you been? We've been waiting."

"Chris, California has the tenth largest economy in the world. What do you think about Californians now, buddy boy?"

I got turned around. My mother had always said she lost her sense of bearing whenever she was inside a building because she did not know which side the sun was on. "I did not grow up on a farm," I said louder than I should have. "Damn this all to Hell. I'm getting out of here. No watch, no nothing. You can all go straight to Hell for all I care."

I proceeded out to the parking lot, and I was watching what was coming my way. It was Jude. I caught him by surprise. He parked right next to me. He was driving a black SUV.

"Well, old friend. We meet again," I said as he climbed out of his vehicle.

"Chris, a pleasure to see you. How you holding up old man?" Jude could not have been more charming. I could not figure out what was going on. I stammered something about being pretty good and then said my friend was waiting on me and I had to go. This freak encounter made no sense.

I pulled up back at my apartment. The damned squirrels were baying and hooting, "Chris, there's a cat down there. Throw a rock, Chris. You have to do something. Survival is a biological imperative, Chris." And then laughter emanated from beyond another building. I could hear it though there was no earthly way I actually could have. It was from the direction of people that were out of sight and beyond range.

I got my keys out, nearly dropping them, and walked into my living room and broke down on the couch and cried. I had a long cry.

Everyone had deserted me and I was sick again. What is to become of me, damn it?"

"You'll be fine, daddy," my twins said.

"Where are you?"

"We're waiting. It won't be long. Trust us, daddy."

I flicked on the television. The commentator on the live news channel began talking directly to me. "In other news, Chris, a Middle East accord has been signed that prevents terrorists from coming into the sovereign nation."

Chris went into his bedroom and got his revolver. He placed it by him on the coffee table in front of his couch, which faced down one wall of his apartment, so he could stretch out and still see the television in the corner. He picked up the gun and popped open the chamber and gave the cylinder a spin and popped it back into place. He stood up and went to his bedroom and got a jacket, and placed the gun in an inside pocket. He went to get coffee. He would be ready for the bastards. They wanted to have fun. He could put a gnat's eye out at twenty feet. He walked along and eventually stepped into the coffee shop.

An older woman sat in a chair reading a book. Her glasses were on top of her head, while another woman just sat in a chair. She looked like she went to tanning salons a lot. Her face had that dried, flaky look, like she had never used a conditioner, and it repulsed Chris. The men without jobs cluttered up the patio area, where Chris had decided to sit after getting his coffee. Chris always thought they had it made. They were there every day, rain or shine with no women, just their war buddies from Bosnia. But then they probably had to beg their wives for money for a cup of coffee. And that was wrong. Chris considered that the language was Eastern European sounding. He thought it was Croat, but was not sure. Anyway, they were never the ones who threatened him. And black men never threatened Chris. They all had too much on their plates as it were. Why bite off more to chew?

So, nothing happened. It was the first time Chris had taken his gun out in public with him. He was not planning to shoot anyone, but would in self-defense. Chris decided while it was daylight he would drive to Daytona, about an hour away, and sit on the beach, and he could come back at night and see Silka. He called her home phone, got her answering machine and left a message that he wanted to see her tonight, if she was willing, and that he would be in around seven or eight, and he would bring takeout. This was what his day was shaping up as. And it was wrong. At least he didn't hallucinate in Croat.

Chris got in his car and drove out I-4, headed east in the direction of Daytona. He stayed on the proper side of the road. He had his revolver still in his jacket pocket. When he got to the city of Daytona Beach, he had a favorite parking spot where he could always park and it was a short walk to the ocean. He took a blanket out of his car and kicked off his shoes and walked in the moist sand. He planned on sitting and relaxing, and as it was not yet spring, there weren't many brave souls on the beach in the late afternoon though the temperatures were mild.

But he could not believe what he heard and saw. The clouds were dancing and actually fighting and turning into likenesses of famous people. There were the Three Stooges, the famous bust of Beethoven, Mademoiselle Blancheflor, and Charlie Chaplin. They all spoke to Chris and he could see their ghostly apparitions in the clouds. Their mouths moved as he heard with his own ears what they said. The last of them was a huge toad with an angry and derisive smile on its wide-open mouth, swallowing other clouds with its tongue as they flew by on the ocean breeze, and on top of the toad was a group of three souls with a jackhammer, hammering deeper and deeper into the toad's brain. Chris took out his revolver and placed it under his shirt, which he had pulled over his head and dropped on the blanket. The nipples of his chest felt so cool and airy. It was refreshing. It was an overcast day, but the sun peeked through here and there and illuminated the underbellies of the clouds. Every bird, every combination of dog and owner, every tourist fresh in from Minnesota spoke to Chris.

"I hate your guts, Chris. You totally screwed up my family with your nonsense. We were betting on Jude. He is much more ruthless than you are." The dog's owner spoke in this manner and then his lab mix sniffed around and took a big dump on the beach.

"I ain't got no truck with you, Chris. Wanna hear a joke, man?"

"Yeah, sure, Chris said out loud.

"Why don't Baptists make love standing up?"

"I don't know, why?" Chris said.

"Because they are afraid that someone will think they're dancing."

Chris laughed. What has happened?" Chris asked the man.

We'all have been activated. Ain't no one from here no more. We all our true selves again, and it's cause of you. Times has changed, buddy boy. And it's all your'n doin."

"We're all aliens?"

"Thas right, even the birds."

"Chris, got any bread…I could use a meal?" an itinerant seagull said. "What do you say, buddy boy?"

Chris sat there a long while. Night had fallen, and it was about six pm or shortly after and Chris decided he had better get home. He wondered if Silka was now an alien creature from somewhere else. Chris motored along and eventually wound up on his home stretch of road and kept noticing on the street blotches of white paint as if they had been dropped from above. "What's with the white paint on the roads?"

A voice resonated in his ear, "they're from the Chinese, Chris. The Chinese fly over in invisible helicopters and paint bomb our streets. I, for one, am getting tired of it. Look at the bike path markings…they're all Chinese symbols. They tell them which way the Caucasian women are. We will all have Chinese blood in another generation. Some of us have turned Chinese already. And we still can't get decent takeout down here."

"I don't believe you," Chris retorted.

"It's true, bitch," another voice, this time a female's voice said. "oh, by the way the KGB is pissed at you. They're going to knock you off. Just thought I would let you know."

"Thanks. I appreciate that," Chris said. "I didn't have enough to worry about."

"They drive all different color SUVs, bitch."

"Who is this?"

"This is your ma-ma. If I hadn't had you, I could have been a Broadway dancer, bitch. But you had to go and commit me."

"I didn't commit you, father did."

"Your father was the only good thing that ever happened to me, and you murdered him. You're such a bitch, Chris. I hate you." She then continued, "Chris darling, you were raped repeatedly when you were a child. It was one of your father's old war buddies. He had a thing for young boys. I knew about it, but I felt it would make you stronger. And it has, bitch. It's made you the man you are today, and we are all so very proud of you. Bitch."

Chris noticed there were sprinklers on in a particular yard as he drew closer to his apartment. It bothered him. The grass might get a fungus that way, running the sprinklers at night. The daylight was needed to soak up the extra moisture or the grass might rot at its roots. Chris saw a group of three women walking down his sidewalk. One of the young women was clearly autistic. She kept touching her eyes with both hands. Chris stared so long, so deeply at the young woman that, as he drove past, he drove a little too close to where they were walking, and he had to snap back the wheel and pop the caddie back into his lane to avoid them. As he parked his car, he witnessed an even more gruesome sight. He noticed a young woman handcuffed to the outer door of another building. He was in great distress seeing this and he called out to her, "Hey you, do you need help?" He wasn't sure if she was real or not. He approached slowly, and then out of the trees a Gatlin gun emerged and started firing off rounds at the dirt beneath Chris' feet. He ran for his building. He made it safely to his apartment and collapsed on the couch.

Chris was creating a scene in his mind. He had stranded his mother on an island somewhere with his father, an island they could never get off of. They would never be able to get off the island because even Chris did not know where it was, just that it was somewhere out in the middle of the deep blue sea in the universe somewhere. The island had green, green grass and was flat without any trees, and his parents had an igloo for shelter, with a stereo inside, two chairs, a television that picked up satellite from their home planet and a bed. "You two love each other so much, have each other, live together, and leave me alone."

"Thanks, Chris. Goodbye," his mother said. His father did not speak.

Chris went into his bathroom and he noticed a fortuitous item, but it was peculiar. And what didn't seem to be lately? He questioned. He had the likeness of Silka in his eyes. Her face was right there in his pupils, and he could see her and talk to her this way always. So, the man on the beach was right. Everyone is activated and an alien now. At least this way, with Silka in his eyes, she would be protected. Chris decided to shave and what ensued was a long conversation with his lover.

"I told you my father was Satan. I didn't know he came from another planet. I haven't read the Bible, so I don't know how much of that is in there. I know he made himself into a snake to poison man and mankind by tempting Eve with an apple, but that is all I really know of the Bible, Silka. You have to believe me. But if he can turn himself into a snake then he surely is not a man or some form of a man, so he must be from another planet."

"Silka, I had a brother and it was his job to dethrone my father, but he got killed at age nineteen in a car accident. My sister is younger and it's not the woman's job. And she got messed up on drugs. I am the one who has to fight because my brother died. And my father is an evil, evil man, but he's not any sort of man at all. Does this sound crazy? I don't think it does at all. I beg to differ, Silka. You have to believe me. You have to trust me."

"Silka, I'm counting on you. I can't get off this rock, otherwise. I have a get-out-of-jail-free card, and I think I can get you one. We can go away together, to somewhere that's nice. Somewhere nicer than heaven. We'll create it. And I'll be fine, I'll be healthy, and so will you, and your little brother when he makes it will be fine too, and the rest of your family when they can make it; we will all be close and close together. What do you say, honey?"

"I think it sounds great too. So, then I am definitely coming back for you. Good, then it's settled. I am coming up to your apartment. I've got Chinese."

Chris walked upstairs to Silka's apartment and knocked on her door, and Hinton answered.

"Who is it, Hinton?"

"It's Uncle Chris," he said.

"Oh. Hi, Chris. How are you feeling?" Silka said.

"I feel great. I've got Chinese."

"I knew you were bringing Chinese," Silka said.

"I just told you," Chris said.

"So, are you sure you're okay?" Silka was a little confused by Chris' answer.

"I'm great, after we talked and all."

"When did we speak?" Now she knew something was up.

"Just now, Silka. Don't you remember?"

"I think you need help, Chris."

"So how is your family?"

"They are good. My brother bought his taxi cab. We all chipped in. I saw him. He moved to Kansas City to be with his other brothers. They'll take turns driving too. It's a good opportunity for them to make some money. I just hope they are careful." It had all been discussed that way as Silka related it to Chris; and that much was true of what she spoke. But she had lied about seeing her brother and chipping in some money, though her brother had gotten the cab and moved to Kansas City. It was through a telephone conversation with her eldest brother that she had learned these bits of information.

"Did you know the KGB is trying to kill me?" Chris asked.

"You're ill, Chris. You need help."

"I figured it all out. My father was a rogue spy for the US government. I don't think he actually worked for them, but he was some kind of misguided patriot and he did various missions that thwarted the efforts of our enemies. He told me he was in Moscow in 1980 with his second wife…you know the one he murdered. He said she drank and spent all his money. He bribed someone I guess. I have no idea whom. He really just got tired of her. He did some sort of mission for the US government in Moscow, and, I think, he placed listening devices in the Kremlin. I'm sure that was it. Or something like that.

Then when I was a child he had me hypnotized because he used me as shield for some mission at some time prior, and he hypnotized me so I wouldn't remember any of the details. But when I turned nineteen in college, he triggered the hypnotic suggestions, I guess, because he didn't approve of my choice of college. My mother had chosen my college with my assistance. So when I was nineteen, I went crazy and in this way he framed me for the Moscow job. But I have never been to Moscow or anywhere else in Russia. I always wanted to go sightseeing, but never did. Then since he had framed me and had driven me crazy, he assumed the KGB would leave me alone because after all I was his son. He didn't want me to die because he needed me on his deathbed. I was a babbling loon, so, I guess, he thought the KGB would leave me alone. And this way, he got off the hook for pulling the job. He made it look like he was never there, and I was. My father was a clever man. But, of course, he's not a man."

"I know. He was Satan and you killed him somehow."

"No, I merely imprisoned him. I trapped him in the jungle, and then just recently I have imprisoned him. I was also raped repeatedly as a child. My mother told me all this, and she was perfectly lucid."

"Really?" Silka said.

"Yeah, I swear. She told me this just today."

"I believe that, Chris. People with your problems often have that in their history. I am aware of that and I never wanted to ask, but I wondered if you knew something like that or not. I'm very sorry."

"She just told me. Yeah, I'm sorry too. I could have been a surgeon or maybe an athlete, but I paint, and that's pretty cool."

"It is cool, Chris. You saw her today?"

"Oh, I didn't see her. We spoke."

"Oh, okay." Silka thought Chris meant by telephone. "Well, it is maybe better to know this." Silka was almost done with her dinner. "The Chinese food was good Chris, but I have a morning shift and I've got to get ready for work. Are you taking your medication?"

"Yes, I am." It was true. I had not missed a dose in days. "Oh, no problem then. I'll see ya." Chris stepped out of Silka's apartment and went downstairs and into his again. He wondered if he had left his television on. He sat and stared blankly at it for a moment and lost his complete train of thought about leaving the television on or off. He thought of Silka instead and the KGB.

Silka does not seem too thrilled with me. She actually asked me to leave this time. She's never done that before. I might be ill, but I don't think so. Everything is coming clear. I wonder what I do about the KGB. My life is hell. Why won't they just leave me alone? Letting me live is the worst torture. I never did anything. My father forged those flight documents. I've never been in Russia. I don't even know how to hook up a bug.

Chris got a beer from his refrigerator. He rarely drank; he was on so much medication, but it might calm his nerves. He couldn't smoke pot anymore; the THC made him deadly paranoid. He flipped on one of those all-night stand-up comic shows, and he could have sworn he heard the comic, a man, say "Chris, here's my impersonation of a SWAT team getting set up. Hut, hut, hut, hut, hut, hut, hut, hut, hut, hut." Chris realized he had not taken his revolver out of his jacket. He was glad he didn't suddenly remember it was there and pull it out in front of Silka again, like he did at the hotel in Daytona Beach. He walked into his bedroom and placed it on the nightstand. He decided he would leave it there for now.

Chris decided to do something he did not do that often, and that was go out at night. He always felt there were scary things in the night, even as a child, but it had stayed with him into his adulthood. He walked up and got a decaffeinated coffee and sat on the patio for a while. He parked himself near the drive-thru camera and microphone, just as a bird swooped down on the telephone line above him. "You've dropped some weight, Chris. You're looking fit." Chris knew, that is to say his understanding was that it was not actually that the birds were alien creatures, even though he clearly heard them speak and could tell it came from them. It was not as the man on the beach that told that joke about Baptists claimed it was. The aliens could see through the birds' eyes and in this way they kept an eye on the entire planet. That was how they knew which people were ready to come home and which ones had to stay. As the rock was a dying planet, there were more and more people allowed on to see if they could atone for their sins from on their home planets. No one cared really what happened on earth. To this point that explained the over-population problem. More and more were allowed on because the earth was going to implode soon.

Chris asked the bird, "Can you see me?" He said it out loud, and there were too ladies seated at a table not far from him. But he was not sure he had done so. Then he drew a whiff of raw sewage so strong and such a stench he almost vomited. He began coughing, and asked the two women seated near him, "Did you smell that?" They got up and walked inside. An Asian woman and her European-appearing passenger pulled up in a mini-van to the drive-thru microphone. It was the pro hitters. Her Scottish partner leaned across into the microphone and ordered an espresso for him and she ordered a green tea for herself. It was about nine pm, and that was not the remarkable thing. They did not even notice Chris seated right near the drive-thru microphone. They paid him no attention at all. They did not even look in his direction.

"We'll have your total at the window," a tinny voice rattled through the cheap microphone. Chris had no clue whom the couple might be, so he was not likely to speak to them and he didn't. Instead, he noticed SUV after SUV pulling through the drive-thru, even at that hour of night. But then some people had worked all day and were just getting off work, and others had fashionably late dinners and were stopping off and getting coffee on the way home. This all made perfect sense to Chris. And he was very glad he had figured out why there was an over-population problem.

What the passengers in the SUVs ordered sounded like complete gibberish and nonsense, as though they had been trained to say those things by the people that worked inside without any of them knowing. One lady ordered a "skinny latte, stirred." Another man and his wife, I presume she was, ordered a signature hot chocolate and an iced latte with three sugars. Chris thought, *an iced latte in winter. It's like wearing white after Labor Day.* A burly man with a tattooed left arm hanging out of his vehicle, in a black pick-up truck with oversized tires, ordered a double cinnamon latte with double espresso shots, whipped and three sugars. It seemed a little insane to Chris. The drink of the man in the pick-up truck cost him over four dollars.

Chris woke up the following morning in a bad mood and rubbed behind his left ear, and sure enough blood came off on his fingers. *The bastards! They were in my apartment. I heard snooker squawk, but I was too tired to get up. The KGB tried to cut off my left ear. I'll shoot the next one that comes in my apartment.*

He would have to go to some doc in the box and see about the doctor removing the ear device. Chris knew immediately that was what it was. It was a two-way. The KGB had placed a microphone in Chris' ear. This way certain of the organization's high-ranking members could speak into another more remote microphone and it would be transmitted into Chris' ear, and as a result he would think he was going crazy. *There's that doctor on Sylvester Street. I bet he'll take it out for me.* Chris dragged himself into the bathroom, but once again he could not face the daily task of getting himself clean. He used the toilet and managed to shave himself. Chris felt proud he could accomplish that much. He had about three days of beard on his face, and many of the whiskers were white.

"You're getting older, buddy boy. You're losing your hair, your beard is white, you did lose your paunch. That much is good. Chris, are you eating? I'm concerned. Don't forget your meds, buddy boy. A day without pills is like a day without sunshine. Did you know that the therapeutic dosage of lithium is very close to the toxic range?"

"My pills can wait…I'll go drive-thru and get some breakfast," Chris said out loud. He noticed his ears in the mirror. There were fully formed scars on both ears on the outside near his sideburns and just under the lobes of his ears. *They tried to cut my ears off. No wonder Snooker was howling last night. I'm sorry, boy. I'll pay closer attention next time.*

"So, the bastards couldn't cut my ears off, so they inserted a speaking device. I'll get that out."

"Chris, rise and shine," a voice with a Russian accent said. "We need you to kill yourself today. How about it, buddy boy? Will you do that for the cause?"

"Screw you," Chris said. Chris put a platoon of Russian soldiers on the deserted island with his mom and father. He barricaded the door so they could not get in the igloo he had given to his parents. "Stay inside you two," he said. "There are Russian soldiers at your door. Let's see how the Russkies like that one. Hey boys, there's Vodka inside. Too bad you don't have any hands." Chris pronounced it like wod-ka, "In the igloo, schmucks. And it's snowing outside." Chris then made the temperatures fall below freezing on the island and the snow rained down in sheets, which picked up more and more and gradually became a blizzard.

"Bastards, you try to cut off my ears again, I'll put your whole fucking army on the island. And I'll shrink them down to M&Ms. The fun-size ones, fuckers."

"Chris, we're sorry. Bring them back and we'll talk."

"Screw you," Chris said. "I've got to go to the doctor because of you."

"This is going to hurt like hell, Chris."

"Just do it. I have an incredibly high tolerance for pain right now. Please get it out."

"There's something in there for real, and it's deep in there."

"I have no idea what it is," Chris said.

"It's a tick, Chris. Have you been camping lately?" the doctor asked.

"No, I don't think so." *They are so predictable, doctors. Camping in March. Yeah, I've been in the Adirondacks. No, the Smokies. I hiked Mt. Everest.*

"You don't know if you've been camping?"

"No, I was up at the dog park and I lay down in the grass," Chris said. He lied. He knew it was a tiny little microphone that the KGB had inserted to drive him crazy. He was allowing for the idiot doctor to save face.

"Okay, I've anesthetized the ear, but it's going to hurt."

"Just get it out, Doctor. I'll deal with the pain later."

He pulled it out after rooting around and going deep in the ar. "I have to get the head or it grows back," the doctor said. "Got it." He dropped it in a metal wash bin. It clanked when it dropped in, so Chris knew it was a small piece of metal that came out of his ear. *Bastards. They broke in my apartment. Colonel, you can have your men back if you'll leave me alone.*

"Agreed. It's General by the way."

"*Who gives a rat's ass. Poof. They're back.*" And Chris took them off the deserted island and put them back in Moscow. "*They can catch a train to the front lines.*"

"No problem, Chris. Thanks. Can you give them back their hands?" The man spoke with a deep Russian accent and a voice of authority.

"All right, breakfast time, doc. I'm going to get sausage sandwiches--want one?"

"No, you enjoy. Let me smear that with a topical anti-bacterial before you go. You know you shouldn't shave so high. You've scarred up the outside of your ears too."

"Those scars weren't there yesterday," Chris said.

"How can that be?" the doctor asked. He was a little mystified by his patient.

"I don't know. Maybe they were. I'll put some lotion on them."

"Are your eyes bothering you? They look very red."

"They are kind of scratchy," Chris said. But he could not allow the doctor to look closely into his pupils because he might see Silka's face there. It's just early morning dry eyes. Unbeknownst to him, Chris actually had sties in both his eyes and as the day wound on, they would hurt him more and more.

"I'll give you some drops."

"Okay, thanks, doc."

Chapter Sixteen

The song by ColdPlay, "Spies…hide in every corner," played on Chris' car
stereo. "Oh what a web we weave, when first we practice to deceive," Chris said out loud
to himself. It was a quote from Alexander Pope's *The Rape of the Lock*. Chris went ahead
and got breakfast, as he had planned. He went back to his apartment to eat and watch a
little television. It was probably past his window for painting. That window usually
opened very early in the morning around five am or so, and only stayed open for a short
hour or two, and then likely he could only accomplish working during that period. If he
managed to get some work done, he felt invigorated, rejuvenated, and could continue
with bright spirits for the day ahead. But it was not always that he could do that. The
juices did not always flow, and if that one percent of inspiration was not there, he wound
up usually listless and forlorn for the day, and needing to wait and try again the next day.
He had finished his painting of himself and Silka, so he decided now was as good as any
time to give it to her. He went upstairs.

She answered her door. "Chris, hey there. Did you have breakfast?"

"Yes, I did. Thank you. I've got something for you." Chris had tucked the
painting and frame around the corner from the door, so Silka would not see it when she
opened the door. It was wrapped in a kind of brown shipping paper.

"It's the painting of us," Silka said. "Oh,my. You're giving it to me?"

"Of course. It's us, but it doesn't look exactly like us. I had to take some
liberties."

Silka unwrapped the gift. She had guessed what it was. "Oh my God. It's
stunning. Oh, my, Chris. Thank you. I have to hang this up right now. How about over
the fish tank? What do you think?"

"It's yours. You decide. I think that's a good place."

"So how are you feeling Chris? I'm worried." Silka called back to him as she
rooted in her toolbox for her picture hangers.

"I think I'm okay. It's been rough weather, but I'm used to that. Creativity is born
of problems. The KGB tried to cut my ears off," Chris said.

"You blew it, buddy boy. You had her on the ropes, and you let her up. What kind
of fighter are you?" a voice said in Chris' mind.

"The KGB?" Chris you're not well. Seriously, I think you need to go into the
hospital. You have insurance, right?" Silka said.

"Yeah, I do. The hospital might be sort of a vacation for me, but I get a lot of
work done at times like these. Maybe you're right. Maybe I'm sick, but I'm back taking
my meds." Chris lied about his meds. He had never lied to Silka before. He had not taken
them in two days, and had grown rather lackadaisical about them. The meds never really
worked fully. They were a Band-Aid for a severed limb that was gushing blood from an
artery, but they were at least a Band-Aid. That's all there was any more: the Band-Aid
method of psychiatry.

"Well, that much is good," Silka said. But I think you need closer supervision."

"I'll think about it. Are we still a couple?" Chris asked.

"Yes, honey. It's not over between us. You haven't done anything to me. I'm just
worried and you don't seem right, and Hinton is acting up again, and I don't know why,

and they don't have a doctor at this daycare for special children that he goes to. And I am thinking he needs a prescription change. It has to be because mom and dad are gone now, but he won't talk about it. And I don't know where to go, and I've talked to them at his center and they can't recommend anyone because they're not qualified or they don't want the liability or their just jerks. I don't know what it is, really. He's been fine at home. A little restless, because he's used to a bigger place," Silka said.

"Do you want me to spend some time with him?" Chris asked.

"No, darling. He's very sensitive to people's energy and I am afraid it is not a good idea right now. And I've got to get ready for my day job. I took a second job, Chris. I didn't want to tell you."

"Do you need some money?"

"No, that is exactly why I didn't want to tell you. Because I knew you would offer to loan me some money, but that has never worked out well for me, so I don't want to do that to us, okay? Do you understand?"

"I think I do. You're a welcher." Chris laughed. He thought it was the funniest thing.

"Right, go ahead and laugh. And I do not welch. Very funny." Silka was not upset. She was smiling. She was glad he had made a joke. He seemed a little more normal today. *Maybe his meds are kicking in again*, she thought. "I hate to do this to you again, but I have to get ready. Keep me company while I am in the shower."

"Absolutely." This was a reason Chris loved younger women. They just acted differently from older women, and though they had less experience and usually were not as wise and often not as supportive, Silka was very knowledgeable about a number of factors concerning relationships. Younger women were often more into themselves, this kind of "me" thing women go through. But Silka had worked through much of that, it seemed to Chris. And Silka had not had that many relationships, but he guessed they were rather intense ones, and she had certainly learned a multitude of things about men.

"Tatianna said you and Chanel got into an argument. Are you two okay?" Silka asked. She didn't mean to bring up the subject. It was an accident. It was a slip of the hip, like a wet bar of soap in a tub.

"Yeah, we're fine. Chanel and I will always be there for each other. We're like brother and sister. We had a difference of opinion and that was all. I have to drop by there sometime soon, in fact. I'll take her some flowers, if you don't mind? When did you see Tatianna?" Chris asked.

Silka made the water hotter and pushed her face under the shower head. She couldn't tell Chris it was at Jude's house because she had told him she had been away on family business. She did enjoy the lake house though. "We went to lunch."

"Oh, how is she?"

"She's fine. Everything is good with her. Your old friend, Jude, was at lunch with her. I didn't stay long."

"He's a creep," Chris said.

"I agree," Silka said. "I didn't really like him. You don't think he is still trying to kill you?"

"Maybe not. I don't know anymore. I have to go."

Silka was done with her shower and the show was over, so she let Chris out and locked the door. Her hair was up in a towel and her sleek lines made her look even taller than she was. She had to get to the grocery store where she was a cashier, and then in the afternoon to the boutique, and still find time to drop off and pick up Hinton, fix dinner, and get some rest. She was tired after the vacation and all that walking around the theme parks, and she had a long day today. Truth be known she was more worried about Chris.

She could get Hinton to open up eventually about what the problem was. Chris she did not know as well. He might keep a lot of things hidden or buried. And for years. Men are like that, she considered. She wanted and needed to help him she felt, but she wasn't sure she could point out to him that he was ill, and she felt he clearly was. He would probably require hospitalization. His actions and speech had grown a little funny and she could tell he was not feeling like himself. But she had to get to work. She had to support herself and her brother and there was no cavalry coming over the hill. She finished up in the bathroom and Hinton was already ready and they walked down to her car, and she turned on a favorite news show on the radio. Hinton was quiet as usual. She worried about him as well.

Chris went back upstairs and decided on a plan. He called out, "Where's my two F-44 Hornets?" The room shone with light that had not been there before. It was a bright light that lit up the room. "You two, my two, are going to become my troops. What do you say?"

"We love you, daddy," the twins said in unison.

"I love you both too. Keep your eyes and ears out for daddy, or whatever you have. You may not be in earthly form. I don't want the KGB getting in this apartment again. I don't want them following me, or my father's men, or anything else like that. Got it, my two?"

"We got it, daddy."

"I love you, my girls. Do you want to play?"

"Not now, daddy. We have work to do. Dream of us daddy."

"Okay," and Chris went into his bedroom and curled up in his bed but he did not dream so that he could remember anyway. He tossed and turned at night so, that he often found it easier to sleep during the day. There were not as many prowlers in his mind during the day. He did not like getting his nights and days turned around. And the scary trailers of movies on television at night upset him, so often so, he would have his gun out and beside him if he stayed up late watching television.

"I wonder if I can turn invisible," Chris said out loud to himself.

"Do it, bitch." It was Chris' ex-wife Alison that persuaded him to try. It was the fifteenth of March. The day Caesar died. Chris woke up in his apartment. The light and ceiling fan were still on from a fitful night's sleep. But the night had been quiet in his home. Snooker had had a chance to sleep as well. He was perched way atop his cage when Chris walked through his living room to fix coffee in the kitchen. "I am invisible for the next twenty-four hours. I'll only come visible if I speak out loud. My two?"

"It is so, daddy."

"But I can see myself still," Chris said out loud.

"You're not invisible to yourself ever, buddy boy. You are so dumb. And I'll figure this one out and I'll still get you. I know all about the ides of March. I was there." The voice was rather nondescript, but it had to be Chris' father. Even though Chris had stranded him on a deserted island somewhere in his imagination, or perhaps it was a physical space and time in the universe, Chris did not desire to taunt him.

"Ok, well, whatever to you, Sir. Chris out."

"Come back here you, bitch. I'm not done with…

The voice trailed off and faded out of its own accord. Maybe that would work. "Chris out." It has a certain ring to it. It had a military tone, one of authority. He wanted to test it again, but he would wait to see if there was another more appropriate moment.

Meanwhile there were two men having a brilliant laugh together. They had checked their post office box and had received from a strange party to both of them, a check for five thousand dollars made out in the name of a business they ran. The business was a sham. The business relied upon one of many websites the two men had going on the Internet. The stranger who sent the check thought he was getting a hit for the money, the pro hitters whom he thought were in town, but the joke was on the man paying for bogus services.

"What a rube. It has a Florida address. Probably some farm boy. It has his home address," one of the two owners of the website said.

"Patsy. Some people make it too easy," the other man said. "Like someone would show their profile on a website if they were a killer for hire. You've got to know people in this world."

"Let's cash it," the first man said.

"Ditto. Steaks on me," the second man said.

Chris went up to his favorite coffee shop, the one near his apartment, and walked in silently and discreetly. No one looked in his direction. No one shot a disapproving glance his way. He was convinced he was invisible. Instead of speaking and ordering coffee, which it might come as a bit of a shock to the girls that took the orders, if he suddenly appeared, he merely grabbed a fruit drink and walked out to the patio with it and without paying for the beverage.

One of the busier gals working the register said, "Did he just walk out with that?" Another said, "It looked like it. Maybe he'll come back in."

Chris did not hear the conversation. He was already on the patio outside. There was no one out there besides him. It wouldn't have mattered because Chris was invisible. He said to himself, "*This is sweet.*" He drank his fruit juice and sat there a long while. It was a warmer day than it had been of late. The fifteenth of March. The day of reckoning. It was a good day to spill some blood. But Chris had almost made it. He would fix dinner or go out and get something and then get a good night's sleep, he thought. Tomorrow if he was still alive, everything would be right with his world. That was a stroke of genius he had, turning himself invisible. He wondered if anyone viewed through the glass, the fruit drink going up in the air by itself and tilting into his mouth, or if the things he touched somehow turned invisible too. That would make more sense, but he had not included for that in his command line. So, he didn't really know. No one came outside to check on him or ask him to pay. He was invisible. They could not see him. No one could.

If the Asian lady and the Scotsman drove by right now, not that Chris had the slightest inkling who they were, he would not have cared one bit. How could pro hitters hit an invisible target? They were not that good. But Chris, of course, knew nothing of the pro hitters. It had never crossed his mind that professional killers were in town because of him. By coincidence it seemed, but not really, more a cosmic moment of timing, Chris wondered what the shots were that fired from atop the grocery store in his direction. Could it be he imagined the gun shots? Were they some sort of backfire from a vehicle or someone operating a jackhammer nearby, he wondered. But the dirt flew up outside the coffee shop. It had to be something, he questioned. Was all this real or not? He could not decide, but he felt a good steak with a baked potato sounded good, and since he planned to pay for them, he said out loud, "good," and he became visible. He walked around the side of the building and away from the coffee shop and toward the grocery store.

"It will all come clear," a voice said to Chris.

"That's nice," Chris said. He was in a good mood and didn't care what the barely distinguishable voice said. It was just a voice among a myriad of voices he had heard and still did. He decided to humor the voices. "That's it. I'll be nice if you'll be nice." Chris was walking across the parking lot to the grocery store having this conversation with himself. He spoke to himself everywhere he went now. A couple of people looked and stared a bit in his direction. Chris could not tell really if they were staring at him, and he cared little if they were. He did a fake tip of the nonexistent hat to one lady, whose gaze seemed more intent than anyone else's.

"How are you, ma'am?"

"Fine," she said and continued stuffing loads of groceries, enough to feed ten families, into the back of her SUV.

"I'm glad," Chris said as he kept walking. "I can always find room for pleasantries."

The lady looked back over her shoulder in Chris' direction. But he went in and bought his steak and potato and paid for them and walked out and back to his apartment. "Fry this up in the skillet, cut up the potato and boil it, like them that way better than baked, and watch some television," Chris spoke to himself as he waited in line to pay for his meal. He pressed on from there and went into his apartment. "I'm invisible again," he commanded, once inside his apartment. *No KGB tonight.* Chris laughed. *I'll sleep on the couch. They won't expect that, and they'll never find me.*

Chris knew why the KGB were sniffing around him. His father had framed him. His father pulled that job in Moscow and then drove Chris crazy by means of hypnotism to make it look like he had been the one who pulled the job. Satan liked very much to get involved with espionage and foreign affairs for world governments. Chris knew he had never been in Moscow and never really cared to go that much. He would prefer a trip to Georgia in the south of Russia on the Black Sea. The hypnotic triggers went off while Chris was in college. Chris' father had sent Chris to a doctor that prescribed something for Chris that went off when mixed with alcohol. It felt like a mind bomb. There was a physical sensation to it, and it was uncomfortable. He could still feel it. Chris' mind blew that same day he took the first pill. He felt like he had an extra dose of gravity, or there were more G forces on him. And his mind was shot. It would never be the same. This was what eventually led to Chris' dropping out of his college for a time, while he completed his tour of a nervous breakdown. And then, while he was still in college, everyone was after Chris again, not the least of whom were the KGB. His father must have peeked around the corner of time to get that one straight or perhaps it went to clever planning. Chris could never outsmart his father; he could only beat him at chess, which says a lot, but not when his father held all the cards.

His father had wanted Chris to stick close by and go to a state school, but Chris had earned a full scholarship to a fine school out on the prairie. He knew he wasn't going to a state school, so he defied his father's wishes and his father got even. It always seemed a kind of harsh price to have the KGB after him since the age of nineteen when all Chris did was assert himself and choose his own college. His father wouldn't just have Chris killed. It seemed he wanted to bat him around a bit like a cat does a trapped mouse. Chris' father set Chris up and effectively got himself off the hook, not that in Chris' estimation that would have made a huge difference. The KGB were quite enamored with Chris' father. They were old friends.

Chris pan fried his steak and sat down to his meal. The television shows were not addressing him directly, but it always seemed the commentators of various and sundry programs were alert that Chris was watching and always tried to put their best foot forward. The beautiful gal on the financial channel always said something to Chris, a word of encouragement or two, but it was past time for that program. Chris called out to his F-44 Hornets. "My two, stand guard duty tonight."

"Okay daddy."

Chris fell asleep on the couch.

Chapter Seventeen

Chris woke up in a puddle of sweat. He had left the heat on too high. The apartment was seventy-eight degrees, a bit on the warm side. It was also the sixteenth of March, but he decided to check the date on his computer before Chris made any formal proclamations of his success in surviving the ides of March. Sure enough, March sixteenth. He was ready to consider making New Year's resolutions. He had been sprung from the hoary pits of his marriage, and met a fabulous new younger woman, completed a painting already this year and survived a final bout of misfortune with his father and his father's death as well. He wanted to celebrate and went out shopping for some spring gear at the mall. It was a huge mistake.

Everywhere he went all the people he talked to, everyone that waited on him, everyone that walked by looked like someone familiar. The girl at the food court resembled Silka, so closely in fact that Chris thought this was her second job and that was why she didn't want to mention it. She was embarrassed she worked at a food court in a mall and it had nothing to do with money. Then Chris noticed it was not she, but a very close resemblance, so close that she could have been a body double, but the faces did not match up. Silka's was smoother and creamier to look upon. She used a lot of lotion on her face. This girl at the food court had a kind of mean and rough facial expression like she had been slinging hash for a while.

The elderly couple seated near where he sat and munched his breakfast looked like his parents. Old balding men with white beards all look the same particularly if they have that bowling ball-shaped tummy. The lady and child at the far table looked like Alison, his ex-wife. A clone of Jude worked at the mobile phone kiosk across the way. Chris was more confused than ever. Everyone had taken on multiple forms. He was surrounded. The coffee shop was the same story. The gals looked like younger versions of Silka or Chanel or Tatianna. Then there was this ringing in Chris' ears, and a voice said, "Your computer has just been updated."

"I see," Chris said.

The cashier at the grocery store looked familiar. Even black women, of whom Chris knew only a few, looked like someone related to Chris' drama. It was all too much for Chris. He no longer had a clue what was happening. On aisle nine in the frozen food section is where Chris lost it. He broke down and began weeping and sat down on the floor, leaning against a freezer case, saying out loud over and over "I don't want to do this anymore." Then he lay on the cold floor in the fetal position, and kept repeating, "It will be all right, Chris." He didn't know if he spoke the words or now the words channeled to him were coming through his mouth. His words, or whose they were, were interspersed with sobs. He had had all he could take. It was the true beginning of the end for Chris. He was not going to make it out of this. He was that sure.

Fortunately it was early in the day, and the grocery store was not too crowded. There were not many that witnessed Chris' shame, but a friendly and clever manager was able to prop Chris up long enough to get him out of the store. He made Chris feel better with a few choice words of his own experience, something about never throwing in the towel, and though very cliché, it was this discourse and the manager's sincerity that convinced Chris to go home and sleep it off and watch a little television. Chris was sure the man thought him a drunk with the three days of beard on his chin and a rather potent body aroma. Chris told the man that was what he was going to do. But he didn't sleep nor did Chris watch television. He stepped into his studio and sketched on canvass a realistic rendering of what had just happened. Art goes on. After a couple of hours in his studio, he called Silka's home phone, not her cell phone because he did not like bothering her at work, and left the message that they should watch television tonight and that Chris would cook pasta and Hinton could have hot dogs if he liked.

Silka called about five and told Chris she would be over around seven with Hinton and that he would like hot dogs. Silka had no clue what was going to happen. It was completely unexpected. As the pair piled into Chris' apartment, they were greeted first outside in the hall with an enticing aroma of pasta and meat sauce. Chris always made it from scratch and it was delicious.

"So how was your day," Chris asked.

"Fine. It went well," Silka said. She was relieved he had asked about her and her day first. He was a very attentive man usually, and by asking how she was, Silka felt Chris felt more or less normal again.

She cleaned up the dishes after dinner and Hinton took his clue to go downstairs and watch his television and get ready for bed. Silka had something in mind, a treat for herself and for Chris. They had not been together in a couple of weeks now. She curled up next to him on the couch. The television was off, and he wanted to know if she wanted to watch a comedy show.

"Sure, for a little while. Come here, you."

Chris sidled closer, but his mind was not at rest and his body was terribly fatigued by stress. Plus, he was now being addressed by the members of the sketch comedy routine on the network he had turned on. Chris, here's one you're going to like," they would say. "Get a load of this one, Chris. You're going to bust your gut on this one."

The bit was two old men playing chess and both men were senile, and while the comedy was rather silly sketch art, Chris listened and found he was ignoring his dinner partner and lover. He had dropped into a day dreamy zone and could not get out.

"You're so tense, Chris. Wow! Feel those muscles," Silka said as she began rubbing and kneading his shoulders and neck. Chris did not even seem to notice what she was doing. He made no response. He had a vague feeling that someone was touching him, and then he wondered if he was about to have an out-of-body experience and whether he would be able to climb back in his body. He went into his bedroom and got his revolver. Silka was terrified. She screamed, "No, Chris. Please." She began crying. Chris shot out the television tube and it exploded and caught fire. He dropped the gun and collapsed to his knees, sobbing. Silka ran and got the fire extinguisher in the closet and put out the fire. She unplugged the television.

"Chris, just leave the gun. I thought you were going to shoot me. I am calling 911 and you have to go into the hospital or I can't be with you any more."

"Okay, I'll go. I wasn't going to shoot you. The television cast members were talking to me."

"Go pack a light bag, and nothing dangerous. I am having the police confiscate your gun."

"Okay, they can take it. It's all a mystery to me anyway. I don't really need it. I have my two."

"Whatever it is you're talking about, I'm sure you are going to feel better soon. I'll be waiting when you get out, okay? Do you trust me?"

"Yes, but I don't want to go. I might lose you."

"No one is going to lose anyone or anything. You have to go. Promise me right now."

"Yes, I promise. I'm going in the hospital."

"Okay. I'll feed Snooker," Silka said.

Silka called 911. "No ma'am, he didn't hurt me. He's sick. He's mentally ill. He needs to go the hospital. I don't want him arrested. He's been talking about suicide a lot lately," Silka said. She figured that would convince the officers he needed psychiatric help, and not a jail cell. Silka was beside herself because she was afraid they might arrest him any way for having a gun and discharging it inside the city limits.

There was a loud knock at Chris' apartment door. Silka let them in. Chris had stopped crying and seemed fully rational. He spoke to the policemen with respect and candor.

"I'm schizophrenic and bi-polar officers. I think I'm sick. I would like to go to Baptist Psych."

"No problem. You'll have to get yourself a new TV, it looks like."

"We'll go shopping when I get out," Chris said indicating he and Silka would be together, though he thought it unlikely. No one ever stays when someone goes through a psychosis. Perhaps one's mother and that is the only person who can handle the stress or help repair someone after the debilitating effects of a psychosis.

"We will too. Now go and get yourself better. I'll find out when visiting hours are and try to visit you."

"That would be great."

The police officers cuffed Chris and put him in the back of a squad car. The police officers were a chatty pair and they were very interested in the fact that Chris painted. One of them played the piano. Chris could not concentrate that well, but he tried. And the officers realized he was under extreme distress until Chris realized he was actually being taken to the hospital and there were no tricks or games involved. He felt a little more assured. The officers walked him into the hospital, still handcuffed and got him a room at the Baptist Hilton, the best psych ward in the city. The clerks processed Chris in, and there he was, a captive. He heard the metal door behind him clank shut. The officers then took off his cuffs. And one of them did a funny thing, which got Chris a little worried. One officer said, "Feel better, Chris." He used Chris's name, and that seemed an unlikely event to occur to Chris. But perhaps not: perhaps he was just being friendly and Chris was being paranoid.

Chris was processed into a room. The room number was 424, and he knew immediately he was going to be executed in the hospital. This room, the inhabitant of it, would be killed. It was the KGB death room, on the more disturbed side of the ward. No one would know he was gone. Silka had done this. It was all Silka who had set him up from the beginning. He thought for a long moment. She had watched him and learned his habits and activities. She knew what became his favorite coffee shop. She moved into her apartment the same day as Chris. He bet that was true. So, they had him under lock and key. He had come here to die after all. The KGB was infamous for taking pretty girls and twisting them and shaping them into the organization's plan and forcing them to do its bidding. The KGB had probably been holding her brother hostage.

They can play a rough game. It was all a deception and if he survived he was not ever getting out. He had no one to call. There was no phone on his end of the wing and the door was locked between the two wings, and there was a brilliant flashing white light that separated the two wings down the only corridor. It was to keep alien intruders that were friendly to Chris' cause away from him. They would be blinded by the brilliant flashing light.

And what was Silka's payoff? Money. And her family, Chris guessed. And she would move out of her apartment and never be seen or found again. Chris would never see her again. He broke down and wept on his bed again in the fetal position. Even though she had done this to him, Chris still loved her. The pain was too much. He sobbed loudly and for a long time. It made his eyes feel better, but that was about all. He wasn't even sure if the door to his room was locked or not. He tried the knob and it opened. At least that much was good. He could move about the ward. It actually was a psychiatric ward, but somehow the KGB had infiltrated. It was like this everywhere anyone went. They were all over the place.

Chris was informed by way of posted material what the daily routine was. He was to eat three times a day and there was a snack around nine pm and then lights out at ten pm. He did not have to go to sleep, but he had to be in his room. There was no counseling for his side of the wing, only a television in the day room. His side of the hospital was for the incurable crazies, but they kept saying he was brought in under the *Baker Act*, and he knew the *Baker Act* had time limitations. They would have to let him out at some point, if they didn't kill him first.

Meds were served twice a day, morning and evening after meals. Chris preferred his as an aperitif. He adjusted to the routine quickly because there was absolutely nothing else to do. He had not brought any books and there was not even a single magazine on the ward. He was going to have to keep his guard up. There were blaring sounds coming from behind the nurses' station. They droned on and were designed to erase the memory of the patients. After a horn cut off, Chris immediately thought about what it was he had been thinking about during the time the horn was roaring, and in this way he tricked the KGB because he would not allow his memory to be erased.

If he played his cards right, he might make it through this, and then he didn't have to see Silka anymore, even if she still lived in Orlando and at her apartment. It was very sad for him. He might have to move. He started to love and hate Silka in the same moment. Days passed and Chris was convinced she had moved away, stolen out into that lonely cruel night and gone who knows where with her brother. She never visited Chris once. The routine grinded on Chris. It was deathly boring. Television in the day room or sleep in his own room: those were the only things to do. He would come out of hibernation for meals only. The staff became fairly polite to him at a certain point. Chris was not sure what had caused the shift. He began to wonder if he might survive the death room after all, but he thought he had been shot with so many cancerous rays this time that he would probably collapse. He hoped his time left was short.

"Come on, my two, it's just over that ridge." The terrain was rugged, as jagged and dangerously sharp peaks shot out of the dead ground and not a stitch of plant life or grass grew. The trees were all dead and misshapen. Their branches turned up toward the bloody sky and the moon shone a pale light over the horrid scene. This was not a land anyone would willingly come to.

"We're right with you, daddy." They trudged on.

The three stopped in their tracks for fear. There was a huge fortification with a twenty-foot-wide moat and a two-headed dog guarding the outside of a large, spiked gate that sealed itself inside of a concrete wall that was twelve feet thick.

"Probability of success, my two?"

"None, daddy." Laughter emanated from not so very far off. It was the gates of hell and inside dwelled Satan, Chris' father. Chris and his two wanted to kill Satan, but there was no way to get at him. Killing the dog, Cerberus, of mythic Greek legend, was an easy thing, getting through the gate might be tougher, but it could be accomplished Chris decided, but the three of them would never find Lucifer in the catacombs. Instinctively, Chris understood the structure stretched far beneath the ground. Chris knew it was an impossible mission. The armaments on the walls were massive, with turrets and towers and thick, massive construction with no windows. It was nearly impenetrable, and then it hit Chris.

"We can get in, but we might never get out," he spoke in hushed tones to his two.

"Let's go, daddy. You're right. It can't be done," the twins said in unison. "You can't fly either," they cautioned.

"So which way do we go? It all looks like wasteland." Then the guns started firing upon the three. The laser-sighted scopes and telepathic missile defense systems, guided by heat and thought to their targets broke loose from the walls and began to crash down around Chris and his twins. Dirt and rock flew up, and the "zing, zing, zing" of unfriendly fire struck horror in their hearts.

"I'm hit. We have to get out of here. I'm going to die," Chris screamed. The laughter grew more ominous and near.

"Look," and there flying through the sky on a winged white horse was Silka, her blonde locks trailing behind her. She had on Medieval armor with chainmail and she scooped up Chris as she landed, and his twins followed hurriedly after. "Get us out of here now," Chris cried.

Then Chris awoke. It had been a dream. But he knew it was not just a dream. He got up and looked out of the window of his hospital room. It looked like a small town scene outside his window, such as one might look upon when witnessing a village in a small third-world country. It looked peaceful at this time of night. The lights had a soft amber glow. Chris wanted to paint it, even though it was his night time, and he did not work with many shades of darker images. He preferred the interplay of light in his work and less somber tones. Then he remembered. He was getting out of the hospital today. The time period for the *Baker Act* was over, even though they had extended it to its full duration. They had to let him out and rightfully so. He felt better than he had all year. He was convinced of staying on his meds and the need for that. He had known better, but a fiendishly clever voice had kept informing him that he was cured. His mind was silent now. It was still. He could see tumbleweeds rolling through his imagination.

Chapter Eighteen

"You're getting out today," the shapely African American nurse said to Chris. He had flirted with her on more than one occasion, and he had found he was not rebuffed so decisively.

"Yee-hah," he said. "I can't wait to get some real food. Some ribs or Chinese or Italian. And go back to work, and sleep in my own bed."

"You think the KGB is still after you, darling?"

"No, I guess they gave up for now. They wouldn't have been able to kill me anyway. I'm too honery." Chris laughed.

"You were fit to be tied when you came in here. We thought we were going to have to put you in isolation for a few nights, but we didn't have to," the nurse said.

"Thank God for small favors. It's the little things in life that matter, like not having to be put in isolation."

"Who's picking you up?" she asked.

"My feet are my only carriage. I'll make it home and I'll build my life back up. I only have one friend, but I got some coin, and a job that pays, and there's Chanel, that's my one friend. But I never told her where I was. I can walk."

"Okay, but I imagine it's a long walk," the nurse said. You can see the doctor right after breakfast, hun. He's already signed your discharge papers."

"I can catch a bus most of the way, I guess. A walk in the fresh air will do me good. Just so long as I get to my side of town by nightfall."

"It won't take you that long, will it?" the nurse asked.

"It's a bit of a hike. It could from here."

Chris met with his doctor after breakfast, just as the nurse said for him to do, and there were no catches. The duration of the *Baker Act* was over and no further petitions to hold him were needed and Chris had experienced the time necessary to prop himself up again. He was thankful. The police had been nice. The hospital staff had been nice to him. His only severe loss this time around was his other best friend, Silka. And that hurt. Everything comes at a price. Everyone and everything. The blinding white light at the end of the corridor had been fixed. Apparently, it was just a loose or fading fluorescent bulb. Chris walked toward the light. The attendant unlocked the double door. "The elevator is in the middle by the nurses' station. Good luck to you, buddy."

The first thing Chris noticed was that the man did not say "buddy boy."

"Thank you," Chris said. He walked out toward the elevator. "So this is how the other half lives." Two of the nurses smiled. One spoke. "Goodbye, Mr. Devin. I hope you have enjoyed your stay," she joked.

Chris smiled. He said, "I have no response to that." He stepped into the elevator as the door opened and pressed the lobby button. A down elevator was a scary notion, but Chris let it go. He just closed his mind to the suggestion and let it go. He was maybe four floors and fifty feet from being a free man. He stepped out of the hospital and drew in a big rush of air. And then he heard something familiar. It was a voice.

"Hi, stranger. Long time no see." It was Silka.

"How did you know I got out today?"

"A nurse told me. How do you feel?"

"Two hundred percent better."

"You want to go home? My car's over there."

"Are we okay?"

"Yeah, we're okay, but it is different, Chris. And I don't know how or why yet, or if it even matters. How about we just love each other? Is that okay?"

"It's okay with me. Let's get take out."

"Let's do it."

.

www.ingramcontent.com/pod-product-compliance
Lightning Source LLC
Chambersburg PA
CBHW050309260626
47156CB00005B/1722